Tiger Lily

Part Two

AMÉLIE S. DUNCAN

DEDICATION

TO ALAN
"I KNOW."

CHAPTER ONE

"LILY," DANI WHISPERED.

I snuggled against her warmth as Dani's fingers traced a circular pattern on my back. My tears had dried up a while ago, yet I couldn't bring myself to let her go. She held me well past what would have been considered polite. My need for touch and assurance outweighed my embarrassment.

We were only acquaintances at best. She was the ex-wife of my now ex-lover, Jonas Crane, making everything bizarre. Nevertheless, I clung to her as she continued to provide the comfort I needed, even if I didn't deserve it. The circumstances that brought her to my bedside in Jersey City hadn't disappeared. She had more she wanted to discuss with me, but if I had my way, that conversation would never happen.

I released my hands from around Dani's slender waist and pulled away from her, allowing the emptiness to fill the absence of her arms. I steadied myself. This was what was left, and what I needed to get used to—feeling empty.

Loneliness was what lured me into accepting Jonas's offer of companionship in the first place. It had been a chance to spend time with him as friends with benefits. But in a relatively short period of time, I had fallen for his company, his attention, and all that was part of his companionship. Still, my falling hadn't been all my fault. His actions had blurred the distance he'd so wanted to maintain between us. It had left me with a deep longing for more.

For Jonas, being with me had been way to assuage his own loneliness after the end of his marriage. His packed schedule as a leader in the business world came at a cost. Dani was now engaged to their friend Alan. His son Paul, now a teenager, grew more interested in spending time with his friends than his father. Jonas went as far as to tell me once he felt like a failure—as though his family had moved on without him.

Looking at Dani, I realized the profound difference between my loneliness and Jonas's. He may have felt lonely, but he wasn't alone. Jonas had what I truly and deeply envied, what I had coveted since the death of my parents. He had a family.

"Your attack…." Dani was saying, interrupting my thoughts.

The words were a jolt to my senses. My eyes widened as they connected with hers. The warmth and empathy I found there touched me, but my conscience chimed in with the painful reminder as to why she was here, rather than back in her luxury apartment on the Upper

Westside. My head dropped. I looked at my hands trembling in my lap—too overwhelmed to still them. The guilt of my lies and deception was laid out before us.

I lied to Jonas and told him I was sick to cover up what happened to me. He, in turn, contacted Dani to check up on me, as he was out of town. She sent me a care basket for a speedy recovery.

A lie that "led to other lies" as my father would have put it. He warned me that as a Salomé, his only daughter, I should never lie. I should hold myself to a higher standard because, eventually, you always got caught up and caught out.

But I didn't listen. Instead, I'd told another lie, texting Dani that I wasn't sick but had merely fallen down, as that was the only explanation that came to mind. Dani proved to be too keen, showing up unannounced and forcing the lie to collapse. There was no hiding the bruises across my face.

I wasn't sick and I hadn't fallen down. I had met up with my ex-fiancé Declan for lunch. He'd taken me to the West Village and hurt me. Declan Gilroy, the same man that I loved, who had cradled my head in his hands when my parent's died, battered me.

I wished I could say that this was an isolated incident, but I would only be lying to myself again. Truthfully, though, I hadn't anticipated his aggression this time. His violence had been sporadic over the course of our three-year relationship, but we were over now. Had been for quite some time. I should have been safe from his outbursts.

While I didn't want to keep in contact with him, he'd made an offer we both knew I couldn't refuse. He told me he had found missing videos and photos of my parents. I searched for years for the treasure he was offering now. I'd been sure it had all perished along with them in the mangled four-door sedan when a drunk driving accident had snatched everything away from me.

Sure, I had other videos and photos. But the ones he promised were the most recent and held the most important memories. They were the remnants of the life in our colonial home on Franklin Street in Quincy, Massachusetts. They captured a time and place when I was utterly and completely happy. I was loved and cherished. I had family.

Declan not only bruised my face, but my heart, leaving me completely empty handed. He told me he had "forgotten" to bring what he promised. When I'd tried to leave, he snapped. Shattering my hopes, I had collected myself and left—silent and empty. I had refused to tell anyone about what occurred and made excuses for him. The bruises would disappear. But the scar in my heart would remain. Protecting him had cost me the possibility of a future with Jonas.

Deep down, I knew it wasn't just my lies and protecting Declan that made me break things off with Jonas. My needs outweighed the perimeters of his companionship. He awakened within me forgotten feelings of happiness and of being cherished. He lavished attention on me, gave me the comfort and touch that I missed, and left me wanting more from him. I'd fallen in love with him, utterly and completely. The pain and finality of his moving out of my life made fresh tears seep down my cheeks.

"But I think it necessary that we at least document what has happened here in order to protect you, should anything—" Dani reached out and squeezed my hands.

"Declan," I murmured. I cleared my throat and said. "He wouldn't hurt me again. I'm fine. Truly, Dani. Thank you for … everything. But I just want to put this all behind me."

It was my automatic response. One I had told myself for years. But now doubt stabbed its needle into my broken heart as I tried my best to convince her. Another lie. A wave of nausea, followed by a dose of self-loathing, took hold of me. Yet I wasn't ready to press charges against him, especially since Declan assured me this time he was going for anger management classes and rehabilitation.

"Okay, Lily, but I need you to do a couple of things before I go," Dani said, calling my attention back to her.

She released my hands and I immediately missed the warmth and strength that seeped through the connection.

"I still think it's necessary that we have some documentation, just in case you change your mind." She held up her hand against the "I won't" I was preparing to provide, standing up instead. "First, a lawyer friend of ours will take your statement and get a few photos of your bruises tonight." She paced a short path along the length of my queen-sized bed. "I'll call Ian."

"Ian Unger?" I blurted.

"Yes." Dani nodded in emphasis. "He's in Tribeca. He'll come over."

I shook my head. "No. I met him with ... Jonas, he's his friend...." I let the words die as my stomach turned over. "I don't want to involve more of Jonas's friends in what I just wanted to put behind me. Please. I'll speak to someone on my own."

I swallowed against the lump in my throat.

Dani's arched brows knitted. "Ian is trustworthy and discreet. It has to be him." She went back to pacing, as if the discussion was over. "Gregor would need to know," she said.

My pulse pounded hard in my chest. "My boss Gregor? Why?"

Dani stopped and stared down at me. "Gregor should be notified just in case Declan comes to your job. So you can be safe. David will drive you to work and—"

"Wait, no, I didn't agree to this, Dani," I said, my voice raising. "I don't need David to take me around. I'm not with Jonas...."

"Even so, Jonas would lose his mind if he knew you were hurt. I know he would agree with me in making sure you are safe." She pushed her blonde bobbed hair back from her shoulders. "As for Ian, he is the only person I know, besides Alan, who wouldn't report it back to Jonas. He has friends in the district attorney's office. He would be good to have in your corner if you change your mind." She lifted her crepe-grey slacks and knelt in front of me. Her brown eyes shone as her tone softened to just above a whisper. "While you still think this man is the person you fell in love with…."

"I know he's not the man I fell in love with," I said, wiping my cheek. "But I still can't do that to Jonas. I can't have his best friends, who he cares for and trusts, keeping things from him."

Lines appeared on her forehead and the corners of her mouth turned down. "You're right. Jonas and I don't keep secrets. So the only way I can make this work, and keep my promise to you, is to have Ian and Gregor involved." She exhaled. "Do those things, and I'll assure you some space."

I folded my arms. I wasn't as sure of her certainty what Jonas might do. But I also noted from the set in her shoulders and the silence that followed, my options were limited. Involving the police could ruin Declan's career and send him to jail. I didn't want to do that to him.

But what about me? My conscience chimed in. I wasn't ready to make any choices right now.

"It's all happening too fast. You're putting too much pressure on me."

"I'm not doing this to hurt you, Lily. I'm doing this to protect you. Even if you're not ready to protect yourself, I am. Me or Jonas. I have no doubt in my mind that Jonas would have this Declan thrown in a hole if he saw your face. He wouldn't be sitting here discussing anything with you. If he knew you were hurt, he would not only act, but completely take over."

I turned my head away, fearful she might have seen the light in my eyes at the thought of being taken over by Jonas. Having the weight and decisions lifted by him didn't bother me. In fact, it sent a thrill up my spine to imagine him taking care of me.

"I see you like that idea," Dani said in a soft tone, drawing me back to her.

My cheeks warmed. I forgot sometimes that Jonas was her ex-husband. Their level of comfort with each other went well beyond anything I ever encountered before, and I wasn't comfortable speaking about my feelings for Jonas with her.

"It's not … I don't know."

"Don't be afraid of asking for what you need." Dani pressed. "Jonas would give you that and so much more. If you let me call him. If you let him he'd move his world for you."

I stared at Dani and sighed. She may have been trying to convince me to change my mind and embrace the possibility of what I could have with Jonas. However, the difference between us expanded critically. Dani was exceedingly wealthy and socially established, which made her not only an attractive partner for Jonas, but also one that fit his world. On the other hand, there was me, surrounded by Star Wars and Star Trek posters, old collegiate books, and CD towers, my most treasured possessions. No social or monetary connections, all of which put me well out of his league.

And even if I was willing to convince myself that it didn't matter, in that moment, I saw in Dani what I would probably never have. Thereby leaving me solely as a companion, never one Jonas would be willing to commit to. Strength. Dani had it in spades. She came in and took over and I quickly acquiesced. I was weak. If I allowed Dani to tell Jonas, he would feel sorry for me and take me out of pity. Until he found another Dani.

"No. I don't want Jonas knowing about this. If Ian is able to meet my wishes, I'll agree to meet with him." I lifted my chin. "In regards to Gregor, he is my boss and friend. I'll tell him on my own. Thank you."

Dani exhaled long and stood up. "Okay. That will work for now." She bent down and picked up the dark Burberry coat she'd left on the floor, removing her cellphone. "I'll call Ian now."

She walked out of my bedroom. I returned to my thoughts and replayed all that I wished I had done differently. I wasn't sure how long I sat there, but before I could decide what I wanted to do next, she opened the door and gave me a small smile.

"Ian will be over in half an hour," Dani said. "I also called David to stop by my place and get my housekeeper, Lin, to put a bag together for you. It'll have some herbal cream to help soothe and heal your face, and a few Chakra cleansing drinks that will help balance you out. There will be sage sticks to burn so you can ward off negativity and … a white candle to leave in your window to guide back those that are lost to you."

I plastered on a smile. Even though I didn't necessarily agree with Dani's beliefs, nor did I understand why she was so willing to help me, I was truly moved by her kindness and support.

"Thank you so much." It popped into my mind how rude it had been of me to not have offered even a glass of water. "Dani, I'm so sorry. Would you like something to drink? I can get you—"

"Don't worry about me, Lily," Dani said, interrupting me and waving her hand. "I can get it myself. You just take a little time for yourself, and I'll come get you when he arrives."

I started to protest, but she walked over and gave me another hug, which I readily accepted. Letting me go, she smoothed my hair with her hands.

"It doesn't end tonight. I want to hear from you, See how you're getting on. Jonas would want the same if you would give him a chance."

I dipped my head down. "Thank you, Dani. But I don't think…."

"Don't right now," she said. "Just know he'd come whenever you're ready."

CHAPTER TWO

A WARMTH WENT through me as I contemplated Dani's kindness. She didn't even know me, but here she was, being nothing but kind and supportive. There wasn't a hint of jealousy at my companionship with Jonas. In fact, she seemed to be encouraging me toward him, though, the thought of being Jonas's friend and watching him with someone else wasn't something I could ever imagine myself being able to do. She was truly extraordinary.

Climbing off my bed, I walked over to the mirrored doors of my closet and pushed the sliding doors back, taking the brush off the top of my dresser. I raked through my long, dark hair, placing it in a high ponytail, though it still fell just past my shoulders.

It was then that I took notice of my appearance. Beyond simply needing a shower after my impromptu workout, I was a complete mess. I decided to get myself at least somewhat cleaned up and presentable before Ian's arrival.

I pulled on a T-shirt over my black tank top, noticing that it hung loosely over my black and red Boston University sweatpants. I was surprised to have found I lost some weight. I crossed the hall to wash my face and brush my teeth, then returned to my bedroom. As I was pulling on a pair of black socks, my bedroom door opened again and Dani poked her head inside.

"Ian is here. Just come out when you're ready."

"I'll be right there, thanks," I said.

A few minutes later, I opened my bedroom door, but was immediately frozen in place when my ears were accosted by raised voices coming from the living room.

"Take her to the hospital to get checked out."

"But then they will report it. I promised Lily I wouldn't push her."

"Why are we keeping this from Jonas? He would *make* her do the right thing."

And there was my cue.

When I entered the room, Ian and Dani were standing next to the couch. He was in full Wall Street business attire—dark navy suit with a tie and crisp white shirt. The set of his high cheek bones, full lush mouth, and wide deep blue eyes that gave him a more feminine beauty, though his square jawline, which was clenched from where I stood, made him masculine and handsome. He ran his hand through his layered blonde hair in an achingly familiar way that instantly catapulted my mind back to Jonas. It was something he did that I found incredibly sexy.

I rubbed my brow to clear my thoughts. "I'm sorry

to involve you, Ian. Jonas and I are not together anymore, but I'll tell him about this fight with Declan when I'm ready."

Relief flooded Dani's face, while Ian's remained skeptical. He took long strides and closed the distance between the two of us, scowling as his gaze roamed over my face.

"Hell, no," Ian said hotly. "This rat bastard goes to jail tonight."

I recoiled and stared down at my black socks. "I'm sorry, Ian, but that's not possible…." I stammered.

I felt his hand brush my shoulder and I flinched.

"Shit," he said, clenching his hands at his sides. "Sorry for upsetting you, but letting this asshole go makes it dangerous for you and anyone else that comes in contact with him. Just keep that in mind when you decide to let him walk around free—"

"Ian. Enough," Dani said crossly. She came over to me and eased her arm around my shoulder, guiding me to the couch to sit down. "This is fresh and she's not ready. You agreed to listen, so let's just get started with her statement and then we'll let Lily get some rest."

Ian walked over and dropped down in my yellow chair. I covered my smile at how odd it looked with him and his black leather briefcase on my pine coffee table. The sci-fi coasters only further enhanced the scene. He pulled out a few legal-sized papers, a recording device, and a camera.

"Most of these are standard consents and agreements

to act in case you choose to press charges against the abuser in the future," Ian said curtly. "I need everything, in your words. The attack as it happened. Sequentially. Any other times he beat you, as well."

I cringed at his words, as they fed my shame.

"Ian. I'm regretting ever contacting you," Dani said with irritation in her voice. "You've completely embarrassed me." She turned to me. "I'm sorry, Lily."

Before I could even respond, he took a breath and said, "I apologize. Again." Ian leaned forward. "Lily, please look at me."

I glanced his way.

"I am sorry if what I say hurts you, I'm here to help. It's just that one of my stepfathers was abusive." He leaned towards me. "I understand you're scared, and I promise even though I'm angry, it's not at you. I'm upset that you were hurt. It's not your fault. Do you understand?"

I sucked in air and nodded. "Yes. Thank you."

"Do you need a few minutes?" Dani asked.

I shook my head. "No."

Taking another breath, I quietly recounted everything that had happened, from the incident a couple of years ago at his house in Chelsea to Declan picking me up from work to Parco's. It all flowed out of me as if I was speaking of someone else. That happened to the old Lily. I'm going to be the new and improved Lily now. Distancing myself made it easier, until I quieted and looked over at Ian, noticing his mouth was pressed into a thin line.

"Sorry this happened to you, Lily," Ian said. "Did anyone else see you after you returned to the office?"

"The receptionist, Olivia," I answered.

"I may contact her for a statement," Ian said.

"I'll give my statement now, too," Dani said.

Ian set his recording device and Dani launched into the text she received from me, and her arrival at my place. I listened as she paused over my deception in telling her I had fallen down. She added some words that were unnecessary, stating that it was common for assault survivors to do so, as if to try to support me in her recount, though I still felt dirty.

After she was finished, Ian turned off his recorder and pulled out a camera. "If you change your mind, I don't care if it's in the middle of the night, call me. I'd be more than willing to get the restraining order and report his assault to the police. It's never too late." He pulled out his card and placed it down on the coffee table. "I'll need your number to get the affidavits back for your signature."

I looked at Dani, who stared at Ian. "You could call me and I'll bring them over."

Ian ignored her and pulled out his cellphone, poised to take my number; I felt compelled to give it to him.

"Now, that's a start," he said. Standing up, he walked around me and turned up the steel lamp next to him to maximum. He pointed over to the wall that boasted only one framed poster. "Stand over there next to *Boba Fett*."

He chuckled and I giggled.

Dani looked at us in puzzlement. "When we met before, Ian mentioned he was a Star Wars fan. Like me."

"Is he now?" Dani said, smirking at Ian.

"Let's take the photos," he said, redirecting the conversation. "Then we'll leave you for tonight."

I rose and walked over to where I had been directed, placing my back against the wall while Ian took photos of me. He was speaking, but my mind was too numb for anything to get through. Posing for a picture made it all the more embarrassing. I wanted to be alone and was happy when they were done and packing up their things.

Dani called David soon afterward, and he came up to the apartment with a bag of alternative health remedies for my "physical and mental health" as Dani described them before they left. I put the Chakra cleansing drinks inside my refrigerator, per her instruction, and carried the rest of the items back to my bedroom. I was exhausted, but still sought a shower before I went to bed.

Crossing the hall, I stepped out of my clothes, climbed inside the shower, and turned the water on full blast. I wished I could wash away Declan and all the dirt that seemed to cling to me whenever he crossed my path, and the guilt of using Dani and Ian, Jonas's best friends, to hide my shame. How low could I possibly get? I disgraced myself, my parents and the Salomé name.

I climbed out and dried my body, then returned to my bedroom to blow-dry my hair. As I was plugging in the hairdryer, I noticed my phone flashing with a new text message. I quickly finished what I was doing, then walked over and checked. My heart skipped a beat as I saw the name flash across the screen. Jonas Crane. I read over his message.

Dani asked me to give you some space and I will, but we're not finished.

A flutter went through my stomach at the thought of seeing Jonas again. In my heart I wanted Jonas not to be finished with me. Pushing aside my negative thoughts and doubts, I picked up the bag and pulled out the candle and lighter inside of it. Walking over to my windowsill, I placed the candle down and lit the wick. It flared to life, giving the room a warm glow as I turned out the lights and crawled under my duvet. Lying on my side, I watched it blaze strong until I finally fell asleep.

CHAPTER THREE

K ISSES ON MY forehead, my cheeks and down to my mouth. I was awake, but pretending to still be asleep. I knew when I opened my eyes I would see his sea blue eyes smiling down at me, along with a smile on his strikingly handsome face.

"Lily, wake up," he finally said and my eyes popped open. "Jonas."

"I knew you weren't asleep," he mocked. "Time to get up. We only have a half hour for breakfast and to get you to work. You slept in again."

"Not my fault," I said. "You kept me up late last night."

His smile spread into a wide grin.

"You didn't seem to mind."

I giggled. "No. I didn't." I cupped his face. "Are you going to wake me like this every morning?"

"I have another idea for the rest of the week."

His eyes took on a mischievous glint. He started kissing a path down the center of my body, pausing at my mound and parting my legs so that he could see the wetness of my arousal. He dragged his tongue through my slit.

"Jonas," I whispered.

My skin heated as my heart pounded in my chest.

"You're so beautiful, Lily," he whispered.

"Come on. This is embarrassing!" I moved to close my legs, but he moved faster, placing his entire mouth over my pussy.

"Oh, Jonas!" I cried out.

"No. Natasha."

My roommate was in my bedroom, shaking me awake. The lights were on and temporarily blinded my vision. I blinked and rubbed my eyes, getting a full view of Natasha's face in front of me. Her knowing smirk sealed my embarrassment.

I glared at her. "What are you doing in here?"

Natasha rolled her eyes. "It's time for our run, silly." She stepped back and pointed to her black and gold spandex outfit. "If you'd move to Manhattan with me, we could rent a place that has a gym and I wouldn't need to wake you up to run with me. Think about it."

"I thought you preferred running outside over the gym?" I said, challenging her logic.

"Whatever," she said, as if that answered everything. "Your face is still messed up. Put on a pair of sunglasses."

"Whatever," I replied, climbing off the bed.

I didn't fight the early morning run, even though I had only slept for a total of three hours the night before, refusing to take anything to help. Dani's herbal remedy must be working. I walked over and took a look at myself. The bruises were practically gone. In a few days, it would be like it had never happened. I could move on.

But I wasn't there yet. So for now, I did as instructed and put on a pair of sunglasses.

I quickly pulled my hair into a bun and put my sweat pants, T-shirt, and sneakers on, then I followed her out of the apartment. Today was a new day and a new me.

Today I was determined to push myself harder than I ever had before. I managed to keep Natasha's pace all the way through downtown and the boardwalk. As we made our way towards our apartment building, I decided to stop at a small shop instead of following her to the end. I dug out the emergency twenty dollars from my pocket and purchased some fat-free yogurt, lettuce, cucumbers and tomatoes, along with Italian dressing. I picked up the *Village Voice* and *Time Out* for ideas on what I could do this week, and made my way back to the apartment.

Once there, I ate a yogurt then walked back to the bathroom, where I looked in the mirror and noticed the herbal creams. Turning on the shower, I wondered what would have happened if I hadn't allowed Dani to find out the truth. I might have been able to keep Jonas and meet him in San Francisco.

I stood under the water and let it beat against my sore muscles, thinking about how things could have been different if I hadn't sent that text. If I hadn't felt guilty for lying and had instead just tried to avoid seeing anyone for a few days, I would still have Jonas and his companionship. But now, I was alone again. I dried myself off, picking up my clothing and crossing the hall into my room, where I placed everything in the laundry.

Walking over to my stereo, I turned it on. Paul McCartney and Wings *Maybe I'm Amazed*. The music filled my room, along with the memories of my first dinner with Jonas at the Waldorf Astoria Hotel. Jonas had remembered me mentioning the music and left the CDs inside a trolley bag he'd gotten me as a gift, since he didn't like me using my Boston University bag for luggage.

I took a deep breath and changed the station to Beyoncé and *Single Ladies* filled the room. Yeah. She's right. If he really liked it, you'd get a commitment. The annoyance blocked my sadness, and I was able to sleep for another two hours before I woke again. How long was this going to last?

I gave up and decided to do some spring-cleaning. I did my laundry and vacuumed my bedroom. This managed to swallow up the morning and most of the afternoon. When I finally sat down on the couch to turn on the TV, the front door buzzed. My pulse sped up. Natasha was off with Ari, so I knew it couldn't be her now.

"Who is it?" I called out.

"Gregor."

I frowned and walked over to the door, opening it up. The shocked horror on his face brought my awareness to my bruises.

"What the hell happened to you?" Gregor asked, his voice elevating.

I locked the door behind him. "Why are you here?"

He folded his arms. "It's the Turner Classic Movie's Alfred Hitchcock *Rebecca* night. I know you invited me some time ago. Before everything happened. But ... well, I hoped we could talk." He shook his head. "Hold up. I want to know what happened to your face. It couldn't be Jonas...."

"No. It wasn't Jonas." I motioned for him to follow me to the couch. "It was my ex. But before you tell me what I need to do, Dani has already taken photos. Ian Unger took a statement, and Declan is off to rehab. So it's over. I'm letting it go."

Gregor cursed. "Still, why isn't that asshole in jail?" He took off his coat and slumped down next to me. "I'll kill that worthless piece of shit. What did Jonas say?"

I licked my lips. "Jonas and I are ... We're not together anymore."

"Is that why he called and tried to push me to move our presentation up to this week?" Gregor asked.

My eyes widened and my mouth parted. "He can't do that. We're not ready."

Gregor nodded in agreement. "He insisted on your presence. But now that I see you, there is no way I'll let that happen. Why don't you take the week off?"

My throat ached. "I can't do that. You need me to help."

Gregor shook his head. "No way in hell will I risk Jonas Crane seeing you hurt and working for me, especially after what happened last week ... I'm sorry."

I crossed my arms. Gregor couldn't bring himself to

mention the kiss. He had been drunk, and it wasn't that big of a deal. But ever since then, he had been avoiding me. "I know. But I need to work right now."

It's all I've got.

He frowned. "Okay. You can work from home on some of the new business we generated from the conference. For which, you will be happy to know, I will be able to swing a bonus. The raise may come later. Mia and Seth will work the Crane meeting."

I shook my head. "I should be there to help. When is it?"

He exhaled. "Not telling you, as you're not invited. And, really, how do you think Jonas will react if I let you work and you're hurt?"

Gregor shuddered.

I made a face, but inwardly it thrilled me to think about Jonas's attention and protectiveness of me. However, I didn't want Jonas fighting with Gregor.

"You're right, Gregor," I relented. "It's better I don't get involved with the presentation."

"Good." Gregor smiled and continued in a soft tone. "Did you have dinner?"

"Yes. I did," I looked down.

I will after he leaves. So it's not exactly a lie.

He hesitated, but didn't challenge me. "Good. I'll send you some work for the week. I want you home for at least a few days. But if you change your mind, you can take some time off. You won't lose your job, I promise." He paused for a moment. "Put some meat on that eye.

The bruises are … God. *I* want to kill him."

My phone rang and I excused myself to retrieve it from the bedroom. It was a message from Ian.

I'll be out of town for the next few days, but when I get back I'd like to meet and have you sign papers. How about Thursday after work? We could make it an early dinner?

I bit my lip. The trip I was supposed to be on with Jonas to San Francisco was Thursday, not that I was going.

We didn't need to meet for dinner. But I didn't want to be rude, so I conceded.

Okay. But it'll have to be an early dinner. I have a lot of work to catch up on.

He texted back immediately

Great. I'll pick you up at Arch Publishing at 5:30 p.m.

I frowned down at my phone. Did Ian think this was a date? And would Gregor let me back at the office by Thursday?

I made my way back to my seat on the couch.

"Jonas?" Gregor wiped his hand across his face.

I shook my head. "Lawyer with papers to sign."

"Good. I hope you do press charges."

I smiled weakly. "It's precautionary. I really just want to move on."

I pulled my legs up on the couch and turned the TV to Turner Classic Movies. *Rebecca* would be on in ten minutes.

"He won't do this again." I promised. "I have something to put on it and it's actually better than it was a couple days ago…."

I stopped speaking, as Gregor's frown deepened. He reached for me and I moved out of his grasp.

Gregor dropped his hand. "I'm not going to lie and say I'm not happy you've broken up. I guess I was a little jealous of you with Jonas, after what happened to Maggie. You're too good for the likes of him. For me too, though I wished things were different for us."

I lowered my head. I could feel the weight of his stare, but we both knew I didn't have the answer he wanted. "I'm not. I don't think of us...."

"You've just been through a lot," Gregor said. "I just want you to know there are people, including me, that think you're amazing and deserve the best." He paused, and I didn't say anything else, as I had no words for him. He continued, "If you need any help—shopping, rides home, whatever ... just let me know. I'll tell the office building to be on the lookout for Declan, just as a precaution."

"Thank you," I said. "I'll be fine." I stood and walked over to the kitchen. "Popcorn?" I asked.

"Yes. Popcorn and wine. What a combination," he said, rising and following me.

He took the opener I handed him and uncorked the bottle of Merlot he had brought with him, pouring a glass for each of us.

We settled back down on the couch and watched the movie, laughing and heckling together. I swooned over Laurence Olivier and he swooned over Joan Fontaine. I smiled at the normalcy of it. Though my mind wondered what Jonas might be up to tonight, I delighted in the somewhat ease Gregor and I shared despite his declaration of feelings. Our movie nights were always enjoyable and I did indeed feel better, but I missed the close friendship I shared with my friend Mary. Perhaps going away for a few days to visit her in Boston would be just the thing I needed to get my head back together.

After a few hours, Gregor left. I returned to the bedroom, unable to still my mind enough to sleep. I started doing crunches, lunges, and running in place until I stopped in exhaustion. I then took a shower and fell face first into my bed, finally able to keep my eyes closed.

I could protect my heart while I was awake, but my dreams were unguarded. They swept me right back to Jonas, where I truly longed to be.

CHAPTER FOUR

THE NUMBER GLOWING on the display of my desk phone forced me to suck in a breath *Declan*. I pressed the mute button to avoid the incessant rings, each one alerting my office colleagues to the fact that I was ignoring calls.

The walls were high enough to give a semblance of privacy, but close enough that I knew what was going on across and next to me. For instance, Margie, who occupied the desk across from me, had a sore throat from her "spirited rendition" of Madonna's *Express Yourself* at karaoke yesterday. And Mark, next to me, had a "secret crush" on my boss Gregor and Seth from Marketing. I could only imagine what they'd learned about me this week, since I'd decided after a couple of days I couldn't take working from home and came back to Arch.

My exercise cure for my insomnia and lack of appetite had left me a bit drowsy. So I'd taken to drinking energy drinks to perk me up in the afternoon. That wasn't good enough office cooler gossip. The only other thing that might hit the rumor radar was that Gregor had started babying me.

Well, not exactly babying. More like sending me out to deliver packages to clients all over Manhattan, something our mail department could easily do. Since I told him Declan was in rehab, and that I hadn't heard from him, he'd had me doing "special deliveries." I suspected the deliveries had to do with Arch's preparation for Jonas's presentation for our bid on the rights to publish his book, though I was being officially taken off the project. Gregor also might have been sparing my reputation. I wore my feelings on my face so he could easily read me. The moment he'd seen me after it happened, he'd known Jonas and I had made love.

Sex. Not love. That was my problem. My heart was lost when it came to Jonas.

Gregor's errands seemed a bit excessive. I had access to his calendar and knew that the Crane presentation had been pushed back a few weeks. But I did as I was told. I actually enjoyed the rides through Manhattan during the day. Although, David, the Crane family's private driver, had been tasked as my escort per my agreement with Dani.

Agreements. Companionships. The Cranes were all business. And that was what I needed to return to. Business.

Between sips of my bottle with lightning bolts on the label, I tucked my shirt into my loose fitting wool pencil skirt, and for the fifth time today, put on my coat. Balancing my handbag and phone, I collected the packages from my desk tray and was ready for my side job as proposal delivery assistant for Arch Limited.

"Thanks for doing this, Lily," Gregor said.

He walked up to me and handed off even more packages. I slid my eyes to the corner and caught a glimpse of Mark's blonde mop. Yep. He had the Gregor crush.

Gregor wasn't much of a looker by conventional standards. His green eyes were a bit buggy, and his facial features sharp. He didn't even dress the part. Take today for instance. He had on a brown checkered shirt and green corduroys. Still, he had that certain special something that made him swoon-worthy around the office. And elsewhere.

I grinned at him. Our Gregor.

"We must be doing great if you can afford to have me spend the afternoon relaxing in the back of a car delivering packages all over Manhattan instead of helping you with the pile of new submissions that came in."

"Not great, but better," Gregor said. "Plus, these are important clients and the personal delivery of our proposals makes them think Arch will go the extra mile for them. That's why I put them in the hands of my most trusted employee, not a guy that's weighed down with a billion deliveries." His brows narrowed as his gaze went over me. "And perhaps the fresh air will do you some good. You alright, Lily?"

I lifted my shoulders and sipped the rest of my energy drink. "Will be in ten minutes."

I laughed, but he didn't join me.

"You look pale, tired," he fussed. "All that sugar can't be good for you."

I exhaled. "Which is why I will be going to the gym at lunch." His gaze softened, and I turned away. "I should be off. David is waiting for me downstairs."

"Yeah. I know," Gregor said, his tone cool. It was a subject we had agreed not to discuss anymore. "How is the Salomé funding coming along?" Gregor asked, changing the subject.

I turned back to him and lifted my shoulders. "Not the best this year. But the bonus helps cover my pledge. So thank you again for that." I plastered on a smile. *No pity.* "Some students have volunteered, but we have a quarter of the participants we had this time last year."

He patted my shoulder. "How about I send an email around the office? That could help some."

I smiled genuinely. "You can't do that. It would go against our policy of soliciting…."

"So, I'll make a new rule. That's what being boss means," Gregor said and winked at me. "Maybe the first week of every month we could allow everyone to send out emails on their charity organizations and information on donating to their causes."

I could see the wheels turning in his head. I stared in admiration. Gregor was a lifesaver.

Although Ms. Parker had mentioned she was able to raise funds through the phone-a-thon, we were still far behind the funding we had received last year. I would have to do something to bring in more money, and soon, or it would be a struggle to continue the program next year. His offer of promotion could be beneficial.

"Thanks, Gregor."

I walked past him and headed to the elevator. My eyes glazed over, not focusing on anything or anyone until I reached the lobby, where Olivia stopped me at the reception desk.

"You had this delivered today," she said with a smile that didn't quite reach her eyes.

Eyes that were studying me. She had been scrutinizing me like this ever since she'd seen my bruised face after the attack. Our once easy acquaintanceship had suffered.

I shifted my gaze away from her and onto the small bouquet of tiger lilies. I quirked my brow. *Jonas?*

"Thank you," I said.

I grasped the little envelope sticking out of the front and walked a few steps away, where I placed the packages on one of the magazine tables in the lobby. My hands trembled as I pulled out the message and read it.

I love you, Tiger Lily. Forgive me. Declan.

My heart constricted at the mention of my nickname, Tiger Lily, given to me by my parents. The name came from a brave and loyal princess that played a brief part in J.M. Barrie's book, *Peter Pan*, which had come to have special meaning for my family. They'd told me I was brave and loyal, and I'd believed them. Until their deaths. Until Declan.

I grimaced. When would he ever leave me be?

"Would you like someone to bring the flowers up to your desk?" Olivia sung out, calling me from my thoughts.

I lifted my chin. "No, thanks. Would you mind keeping them down here?"

"I can put them in the conference room on the third floor if you'd prefer?"

We looked at each other and in that moment I felt understood. Less alone.

"Yes. That would be great."

I collected the packages and braced myself for the cold weather as I left the building. Still, I shivered. The icy blast of air hit my face and stole my breath. New York was still in the midst of winter weather and, from the grey clouds overhead, maybe more snow. I shook my head as I walked across the stone courtyard, passing a couple clusters of smokers from the offices who shivered without coats in front of the metal caddies outside the building. They were crazy to stand out in this freezing afternoon. I noticed the Bentley waiting for me at the curb. David must have not yet caught sight of me, or he would have been out to greet me.

We had our own uneasy relationship. From the past, he had been Jonas's personal spy, watching over me. Now, Dani Crane had placed him in the position as co-conspirator, watching over me once more, only now not telling Jonas what was going on. This made things uneasy for both him and me. In the last week, I had found my bruises gone, but the stain of them still clung to all who had seen them.

Closing in on my goal, I caught movement fast approaching out of the corner of my eye and paused. What filled my vision made my body tense and my mouth go dry.

Declan's beefy frame was bounding up to me. His wispy strawberry blonde hair was messy around his face, and he had stubble on his round chin. He wore a checked shirt and dark slacks. He never was one to care too much about his appearance, but something was different. Alarming. The steel calm he had on approach had my hair on end. Then realization hit me. For the first time in all the times I'd encountered him, and even the times he'd physically attacked me, I was actually scared of him.

"Where the hell have you been?" he asked, his voice elevated. "I called your phone a bunch of times, but it just goes dead. Did you block me? I can't reach you at work. I came all the way up here and delivered the flowers myself, but I wasn't allowed inside the building."

I backed up from him, my arms crushing the packages. "You're supposed to be in rehab."

"Rehab?" He looked puzzled, as if I had spoken a language he didn't understand. But then realization came back and he rolled his eyes. "I have a business to run, remember? I can't be taking off work for nonsense. I don't have Daddy and Mommy's life insurance to fill in the gaps."

"I don't want to hear it."

My voice came out louder than I meant for it. This being New York, the people on the sidewalk glanced at us, but kept walking.

I turned back to Declan and glared. "You promised you were going to get help this time."

"For what?" Declan asked, smirking.

"For hurting me for starters." My lip trembled. "You beat my face—"

"Stop being dramatic," Declan said, cutting me off and taking a few steps closer.

I quickly backed up against the side of the car, just as the driver side opened and David rushed out. He wasn't beefy like Declan, but one could tell he had an impressively solid frame in his dark suit.

I turned back to Declan. "Just go away," I hissed. "I never want to see you again."

"You alright, Ms. Salomé?"

David started collecting my things and placing them in the trunk, though his eyes were fixed on Declan.

"Yes. He was just leaving," I said.

"You don't mean that." Declan eyed David coolly and dropped his hands at his sides. "I said I was sorry, Lily. I was only upset at you for being all snotty when I saw you over lunch. I sent you flowers, photos, and everything so I already more than made up for it."

I shook my head. "Not nearly enough. Why don't you just move on and leave me alone?"

"Oh, so you can get that rich guy?" Declan asked,

gesturing towards the car and laughed. "He could easily get a supermodel. Do you think you could ever compete? Trust me. You can't."

I could see the pleasure in his face as he watched mine crumble. My heart ached. I wanted to hurt him back.

"People know. The receptionist saw my face after what you did. My boss saw, too. They don't want you near the office."

"You better be lying." The smile on his face evaporated as he met my steady glare. "What did you tell them?"

I stood tall, but my legs jittered. "They know enough to not want you here." His look was lethal, and I ebbed away from him. "I blocked your phone number, too. So stop trying to reach me. Stay away from me." My voice wavered. "I don't want to see you again."

"No way would you tell anyone. I know you," he said, and I didn't correct him. He stepped closer to me. "You know I love you and I never meant to hurt you."

David came around to the sidewalk and stood next to me.

He glared at Declan. "I heard her ask you to leave. Now leave."

A trace of fear appeared, but instantly melted away from Declan's face. "Get your ass back inside your fancy car. This has nothing to do with you." His face contorted into a sneer as he looked back at me. "I came all the way over here for you and you treat me like this? You're going to regret this, Lily."

"Are you threatening her?" David asked. "I'll call the police."

His eyes flicked to me.

"I promise, you'll regret this, Lily," Declan said, backing away. "This stooge won't be around all the time."

He muttered as David moved to the door to hold it open for me. Declan took out a cigarette and strolled away.

I knew he wouldn't stop. I looked up at David, and could feel his disapproval. Though he didn't say anything to me as I sat down inside the car, we both knew he was going to report back to Dani.

"I'll take care of this, David."

I could see the doubt on his face. Even I doubted myself, but I had to do something. Declan didn't look good. Something was more off than usual. Why was he coming around now?

In the six months since we'd broken up, he had never called or anything. The second he witnessed me out and talking with Jonas, he started appearing, calling, and sending gifts. He'd given me the impression he was pursuing me again. Yet, this time, his actions were absent of the love and kindness that had won me over to him before.

"He won't stop," David said as if he plucked the thought from me. "His behavior was hostile. I'm very concerned. I'm calling Ms. Crane."

I dropped my head. "I understand … Please tell Dani I'm contacting Ian and to please hold off until she hears from him."

David nodded slowly and closed the door. Shaking, I typed out a message to Ian Unger.

I'm ready to press charges. What do I need to do first?

CHAPTER FIVE

MY APPOINTMENT CALENDAR buzzed, alerting me that the workday had ended, though I didn't need a reminder. My mind was still on Declan and our encounter in front of the building. That, and my subsequent conversation with Ian Unger in which I had agreed to go to the police station to report Declan. The fear bubbling up inside me was overcome with sorrow as my mind played over all the good times we had shared in our relationship, almost to the point of making me want to call Ian and cancel.

Pushing that thought away, I turned off my computer, packed my things and headed out of the building. I found Ian waiting for me by a Mercedes SUV. He was dressed down—wearing a black sweater, and from what I could see, tight denim jeans that hugged his long, lean legs just right. He pushed his blonde hair back from his face, showing off a handsome profile.

I walked up and awkwardly accepted the surprise brush of his lips against my cheek. A crease appeared, showing off a set of dimples that made him look even more appealing. Not that I was interested.

"Good to see you, Lily," Ian said.

His hand reached for my waist as he helped me climb into the backseat. Not that I couldn't have handled that on my own. At almost five foot seven, I was tall enough to navigate climbing into an SUV.

"Thanks," I muttered.

I moved close to the window seat and buckled up. Ian let out a laugh as he settled down next to me. My legs started to jitter, and his mood took on a more serious tone, which I found comforting.

"We'll go to the police department downtown and get the restraining order," Ian said. "While we're there, we'll get some of the paperwork I brought with me for you to complete."

I nodded rapidly, as a shudder went through me. "What will happen after that?"

"Not much, I'm afraid," Ian said bluntly. "At least, not for a while. But it's a step in the right direction. Best case scenario, he will be arrested."

I trembled. Declan had worked hard over the past five years to build up his import/export business. It was an effort my parents had admired in him, and one I supported by helping him when I could during our relationship. His whole life was invested in that business. If he lost it, he'd be financially ruined, or worse. I couldn't do that to him.

"I don't know about that. I just want Declan to leave me alone. I don't want him to lose his business or to destroy his career."

"He should have thought about that before he hit you. He had to have known that was against the law, but he did it anyway, and risked suffering the consequences. Leaving him alone is as good as leaving him open to do it to someone else," Ian said. "Besides, what about your career and safety? Do you honestly think he cares about that?"

I stared out the window at the passing traffic and thought about Ian's words before answering. No. Declan didn't care. And his chaotic behavior this afternoon left me without doubt he would continue to hassle me.

"No. You're right. But it's hard to think he doesn't … care about me."

"You're doing the right thing, I assure you," Ian said, clasping my hand. "You're not alone, either. You have Dani and me on your side."

I turned my lips up. "Thank you both," I said, easing my hand away.

A smile spread across his face. "You seem to take delight in punishing those you deemed guilty. Why didn't you go into criminal law?"

"Money," Ian said, giving me a dimpled smile that had me smiling back at him.

"Duh," I said, and we both laughed.

"If you feel unsafe, I can have my driver take you around and get more security for you," Ian offered.

"Well, Jonas … I mean, Dani, has David transporting me for now. But I can't have him forever."

"You would if Jonas had his way," Ian said under his breath. "If you don't want David to take you around, my offer stands."

The mere mention of Jonas had my heart aching. I swallowed hard and turned my head, though I felt Ian's gaze on me as I stared at my hand on the window panel. The cold soaked in, cooling off my heated skin.

"Did you see Jonas in San Francisco?" I asked, just above a whisper.

"Yes, I did see him ... and Melissa Finch. Do you know Melissa?"

My pulse sped up as my stomach turned over. The way he said "Melissa" had my Spidey senses firing off "danger ahead." Do not ask, my head begged my heart. But I ignored it and asked anyway.

"No. I don't. Should I know her?"

"Melissa Finch is an heiress to Arthur Finch Construction, which builds all over the world. She's also a psychiatrist, but I suppose you haven't run into her here. She lives in Dallas."

We both knew Jonas was based in Texas, and from Ian's facial expression, I gathered he wanted to say more. I didn't want to think of Jonas with Melissa or anyone else, so I tried to steer our conversation sideways.

"So, how was the conference?"

Ian gave me a sympathetic look. "The conference was good. As for Melissa, she was there with Jonas. You mentioned you broke up, I assumed that was the reason?" he inquired.

Why is he pushing this? I didn't want to know.

"No. Oh. I didn't know." I tried to stop the twitch in my face. "It's fine. I'm happy for him," I lied.

I took in a short breath and leaned my head against the window, soaking in the cold again to cool my hot skin, as I tried to piece myself back together after hearing Ian's news. I'd broken off the companionship with Jonas and in just one week, he had replaced me.

What did I expect? He was gorgeous, rich, and an eligible bachelor. He could get anyone he wanted, just as Declan had said. Why would he waste his time with someone like me?

"I'm sorry, Lily. I didn't mean to upset you," Ian said, softening his tone in response to the crestfallen expression on my face. "For what it's worth, I think Jonas is making a big mistake. If it was me, I wouldn't let you go so easily."

Easily. *Easily replaced.* The words stung, but from what I was coming to know about Ian, he wasn't trying to hurt me. I supposed he was merely providing a dose of reality served up New York City style. Nevertheless, his words bit through the remains of my self-esteem.

Before the tears could begin flowing, the car stopped in front of the downtown police station, though I didn't want to go there or be here at this moment. I wanted to be alone to lick my wounds and try to process the fact that Jonas had moved on from me. But I needed to settle what I had come for, which would require me to be brave. I needed to follow through on my quest to get rid of what was blocking my progress on becoming a new and improved Lily. I needed to press charges against Declan.

Standing in front of the building, an uneasiness settled over me. The dated architecture of the building, along with a swarm of blue uniforms amidst the less than desirable clientele had me thinking *criminal*. It was what my father would have classified as "a place best avoided."

It wasn't that my parents and I didn't respect the police for their bravery and protection. It was just that we had our own prejudices against those needing their services, namely that they were categorically troubled or in trouble. My father would have been ashamed to see me here.

My mother, who went through the foster system in Dorchester, Massachusetts and was quite familiar with both the troubled and those in trouble, went to great lengths to ensure my world never brushed against either one. I surely hadn't wanted to ruin her suburban utopia in Quincy by telling her that her daughter was being hurt by her then-boyfriend. I hadn't ever wanted her to know that the world she had worked so hard to create, along with her only daughter, wasn't perfect.

Sweat coated my body and my heart rate elevated as I placed my items on the security conveyor belt in the lobby. I couldn't help but ponder the irony of the troubled and in trouble. It occurred to me that I was, then and now, both.

Going to the station with Ian had turned out to be a

blessing, as he was able to guide me through the process and paperwork needed to file my initial criminal complaint against Declan. He handled most of the discussion. When a niggling of guilt gripped me, I only had to look at the photos of my injuries being placed in the file before me.

At the end, I was assigned a detective and a case number. The smug look of satisfaction on Declan's face that I had witnessed earlier, when he sought to crush my spirit, also gave me the added strength to persevere in my pursuit of finally closing the door on this relationship.

I took in a deep breath of the chilled air as we stood on the sidewalk in front of the building. "Thank you, Ian. I truly appreciate all your help. We haven't discussed legal fees…."

Ian smiled at me. "Dani would kill me. Besides, I barely did anything. I will also be connecting you to a friend, Diane Langston. She's a criminal lawyer that will help you from here on out. She's top of the line, but does pro-bono for … cases like yours."

I curled my chin under. "For poor women in trouble."

Ian folded his arms. "No. For brave women unfortunately linked to scumbags."

I giggled. "Is that your professional opinion, Mr. Unger?"

"Yes, Ms. Salomé," Ian said.

The car pulled up.

"I'm going to head home," I said, pulling out my

subway pass. "Thanks again."

"I'm, of course, giving you a ride home. As well as dinner," Ian said. "You do remember agreeing to dinner tonight?"

"I'm actually exhausted."

I did remember, but I wanted to be alone to process. Seeing the disappointment on his face, however, I felt instantly guilty.

"But, well, maybe something light?" I added.

"Okay." He grinned. "How about *Per Se*?"

I giggled at the impressive and pricey eatery. "Look at me? I'm hardly dressed for that place."

I motioned towards my pencil skirt and loose shirt, and lifted my ballet flats. Ian's gaze was hot on me as he moved over my body and back to my eyes.

"You look beautiful."

My face went hot and I dipped my head. "Ian, I don't know what to say."

"You don't have to say anything. I just wanted to be clear on my thoughts about you." His lips curled up. "But we'll skip *Per Se*. How about burgers? Would that be better?"

I turned my lips upward. I didn't know what to make of his compliments, but perhaps a bit of friendly company would do me good.

"Sure."

Ian chuckled. "That's better."

He placed his hand on my lower back and helped me inside his SUV. This time I let him. Ian rattled off a place I had never heard of and the divider window rose. His phone buzzed and he spoke to someone else as we sped through downtown towards the village. I turned my phone back on and found voice messages from Dani and Mary. I played Dani's first.

"David called and told me what happened. Ian told me you were going to press charges. I know this is a huge step, and I just want you to know I'm here if you need someone to talk to. Jonas is, too."

I swallowed. They were both extending friendship. I was still unsure about Dani, but now that I knew Jonas was with Melissa, I wouldn't be contacting him anytime soon.

I quickly sent a text to Dani.

You've helped me plenty. Thank you again.

I next played the message from Mary.

"Are you still in San Francisco? I'm up to my ears with papers right now, but I'm not too busy for my best friend."

My heart constricted. Mary. I needed to tell her the truth. Keeping this hidden from her, and everyone close to me, had always been hard. But now I felt especially compelled to tell her. Although we lived away from each other and had been moving in different directions since college, she was still my closest friend.

I had always justified not telling her because I feared she'd pressure me to end things with Declan. Once Mary set her mind on something, she was relentless. But I also knew she would be crushed by my secrecy. She thought of me as I did her, as a sister. I didn't know what I was going to do. Truly, I couldn't bear her disappointment.

The car stopped, bringing me away from my worries. My jaw unhinged as we got out and stood before the building. The entire space was steel and glass, with a large saucer spaceship coming out of the front of it.

"Ian. I didn't know about this place. Is this new?"

He chuckled. "I thought you would like this, though I hope you'll let me take you to *Per Se* next time," he said confidently, holding the door open for me.

Maybe, I thought as I walked in and marveled at a replica of the Dr. Who Tardis in the corner, as well as photos from various sci-fi movies. The hostess approached us dressed like a steam-punk alien. She led us into one of the circular booths in the middle of the restaurant and left the menus with us.

"This is great," I said, looking around the restaurant at the patrons.

They were a great mix of trendy hipsters, steam punks, and families. Ian reached over and squeezed my hand.

"You're shaking," he said.

"I didn't realize."

He released my hand. I took a few deep breaths until I calmed down. *Breathe*, I thought, and my mind wandered over to Jonas and our Tantra yoga session from a few weeks before. I attempted to hide my facial expression, no doubt a goofy grin, by picking up the water that an alien had dropped off and drank it down.

"What are you thinking?" Ian asked, a broad smile appearing on his face. "Whatever it is, please share."

My skin heated. "Uhm. Sorry. It was nothing," I stammered.

He chuckled. "Well, whatever it was, keep it up. That look on your face is almost as lovely as your smile."

He gave me his own dimpled grin.

I blushed all the more. "So, Ian, did you grow up here?"

"Here and Connecticut with my brother and sister. I went to Yale, and then rebelled, as it was my stepfather's alma mater. From there, I went to Harvard Law. After that, I moved to New York City and worked in corporate," Ian said. "You?"

Glancing over at him, I found he was gazing intently at me. Once again, I had been spending time with a man well above my pay grade that I would never have. Was he considering me for a sexual companion, like I'd been to Jonas? No thank you. Exchanging one man for another was outside my level of experience.

I cleared my throat and said, "Boston, Quincy with my parents … then Boston University, and New York. Then I started working with Arch."

He nodded. The waitress came by for our orders, and I picked up the menu.

"I'll have a black hole three bean soup, and salad," I said and handed the menu to the waitress, bracing myself for Ian to protest my choice as Jonas would have. But he didn't.

"Saucer burger, fries, and a chocolate shake." He leaned over close to my ear. "You must try the shakes, they're better than that thought you were having a minute ago."

I grinned. "Alright. A small vanilla shake."

"So, you were living and came from Massachusetts? Why didn't you return to Boston after Declan broke things off?" Ian asked.

My smile wilted. Ian knowing the darker parts of my life left him privy to things I didn't care to discuss with anyone.

"Well, after my parents died, I never felt like I had much to go back to. I had my best friend Mary, but she's doing a master's degree at Boston College. I liked my job at Arch and my apartment in Jersey City. So I stayed."

Ian's seemed to contemplate that for a moment. "I just assumed it would be difficult to start over in an unfamiliar city, but let's talk about something that will bring back your smile. So, what did you think of Star Trek's *Into the Darkness* in comparison to *Wrath of Khan*?"

I laughed. "My friend Mary has a whole fifty-page paper she wrote in her spare time on just that topic. I'm not an old school snob. I love the new Star Trek movies. You?"

"I did, too. But nothing beats William Shatner screaming 'Khan!'."

We both laughed.

"So besides science fiction, what do you enjoy doing?" Ian asked.

The waitress returned with our food and I used the delay to think of something interesting that didn't involve Declan or Jonas.

"I try to help with an art week for children that my mother established called Salomé Love Legacy. I read, and watch old movies."

I shrugged and took a sip of my shake and moaned. It was heaven.

"Sounds good." Ian cleared his throat. "What do you do for fun besides watch movies? Do you like to dance?"

"Well, not formally," I said between bites of my salad. "I used to enjoy live concerts in college. A few nightclubs, but it's not really my scene."

He nodded and ate his burger. "Well. I've been invited to the Finch Fanatic Shimmy under the Stars Gala Fundraiser. Say that five times fast." He gave me a dimpled grin. "It's really a great night out and a good cause. Would you go with me?"

I hesitated, unsure of what to say. I wasn't over Jonas, and with all that was going on, the last thing I wanted to do was start something new, especially since I had hoped Ian and I could be friends.

"So, what's your answer?" Ian asked and I realized it wasn't the first time.

"I don't think I want to go. Thanks."

Silence fell between us. I looked up from my soup, noticing Ian's disappointed gaze, and instantly felt guilty. *It's only a dance, so why not?*

"Oh. Okay. Sure."

A grin spread across Ian's face. "Good girl."

"Never call me that. Please," I huffed.

"Alright."

He laughed and I laughed, too. When I stopped, he held a fry to my lips and a pang went through me at the thought of Jonas feeding me.

I took it in my hand. "Thanks."

I plastered on a smile and ate it.

His gaze lingered on my mouth then met my eyes. "So, it's a date."

CHAPTER SIX

"**Y**OU CAN FIT it," Natasha said.

Her tone ebbed with surprise, as I easily zipped up the back of the black and silver gown I had borrowed from her for the gala event. I had spent most of that morning at Bliss Spa getting a wax, manicure, and pedicure. Since Dee was on vacation, I was able to get his second in command, Marco, to put my hair up in a beautiful French twist. He had even managed to cover my dark circles with "Tim Burton-esque smoke eyes." I was called every gorgeous, gothic woman Marc could think of on my way out the door. It didn't give me the full esteem lift I would have gained from Dee, but fitting easily into one of Natasha's designer dresses certainly helped.

The black-jeweled gown accentuated my curves, but was modest enough to make me comfortable, except for the lace thong that I wore underneath. The thong was still better than Natasha's recommendation of nothing at all. My favorite part of the outfit was that my mother's diamond and silver necklace still looked fine with this dress.

As I stared in my mirrored wardrobe, I couldn't help but recall the symphony Jonas took me to a couple weeks back. I had spent that night in his piercing blue gaze, with rapt attention on every little thing I did. His lean muscular arms had comforted me whenever I needed him. God, I miss him.

The front bell rang.

"Get your coat and clutch. Put on the heels," Natasha barked out her orders. "You should have bought a new pair of shoes. Did you see the salt on the sidewalks, silly? These are black silk," she scolded.

"I'll be careful," I promised as I slipped them on.

I exited my bedroom and sought out my handsome escort, Ian Unger. He had on a black tux. His hair was neatly styled back from his face, showing off his high cheekbones. His eyes glimmered and a smile spread across his face as I came into the room.

"You look beautiful," Ian said.

I blushed. "Thank you. So do you."

He surprised me by leaning down and placing a light kiss on my cheek. "Let's go. Nice meeting you, Natasha."

"Likewise," Natasha purred.

She frowned when Ian's focus returned swiftly back to me. He clasped my hand and we walked out of the apartment building, climbing into the waiting limousine that took us to the New York Pavilion for the gala event.

As we pulled up to the curb, I was in awe. The three story neo-Romanesque building lit up like the night sky.

There were three rings of fire with light sparkles set in front of a large sign displaying the years dance theme: Finch Fanatic's Shimmy-ring Stars. We moved across the stone walkway. Once we handed over the golden ticket, we entered the star-studded foyer where celebrities and socialites mixed with the wealthy and elite. I clasped tightly to his arm, as Ian walked with confidence to the table seating area for the dinner and introduced us to the two other couples at our table.

Despite initially feeling out of place, I eased a bit as the food and drinks were served and we all settled into polite conversation.

After the meal, we watched a dance group dressed in clothing replicating the last fifty years of dance crazes. It culminated in Mark Ronson's *Uptown Funk,* at which point we were all invited to join in. I was surprised when Ian grabbed my hand, and we danced together with those few willing souls that stepped out in the center.

Dancing was always a good stress reliever for me in the privacy of my bedroom. I wasn't as sure of myself in public, but what I found was that I needn't have worried. Ian had moves that surprised me, expertly maneuvering us around the dance floor. The crowd gave us room and encouragement. At the end of the song, Ian pulled me against his hard body as claps exploded around us. It was the perfect moment for a kiss, which he went for. With the pressure of the captive audience, I accepted by offering pressure against his lips, but not deepening it. I then moved my head and took a step back.

Ian lean next to my ear. "I've been wanting to do that since the moment I met you."

I touched my lips in surprise, though I knew Ian wasn't hiding anything from me. I also knew that he was moving too fast and far ahead of me. Walking in front of him, I felt the faint trace of his hand along my lower back as we made our way to our seats. Too much indeed.

"You're a great dancer, Lily," Ian said.

I shrugged. "Hardly. You're like Justin Timberlake."

He laughed and I joined in with him, unknotting the muscles I was tensing.

"Anyway, I enjoyed that," he said, lightly touching the side of my face. I moved my face and picked up my wine, taking a sip. A central stage lit up, and a couple took their place in front of the microphone.

"Good evening and thank you all for attending the 15th Annual Finch Fanatic. I'm Arthur Finch, and this is my fiancée, Rita Wallis."

The attendees started to cheer and clap.

"Finch Fanatic raises money for national charities to help children in need and combat poverty. Our last event raised over five million dollars. That's lunch money for some of you. There has been a change in the presenters this evening. An honorable and pleasured addition to our foundation has graciously agreed to announce our list of charities that we will be sponsoring this year. It is with honor and pleasure I introduce a name synonymous with business as well as philanthropy, Jonas Crane."

My eyes widened as my heart beat to a staccato pulse.

He's here? I looked over at Ian and saw he was as surprised as me. Jonas walked onto the stage and everything else disappeared. One word sprang to mind. *Stunning.* His looks were mesmerizing and combined with his presence, he outshone all those around him. He was dressed in a designer tux that fit his lean muscular frame beautifully. His dark, wavy hair hung longer than I remembered and swept back from his chiseled face. But what made me truly catch my breath were his sea blue eyes that moved over the crowd. The eyes that bore into mine in my dreams. Then there were the sensual lips that I remembered touching all over me. His eyes flashed on me, and a trace of a grimace formed, but instantly morphed into a broad smile, showing off his perfect set of teeth.

I, like the crowd, couldn't look away as he took the podium. Before he could speak, a statuesque buxom blonde in a gorgeous blue gown came up to him and planted a kiss on his cheek. I knew before Ian whispered to me that she was Melissa Finch. Her head tilted upward, showing her perfect profile and the pearly white smile that had a pageantry-winning lilt to it. I had no doubt that if she had ever been in one, she would have been the winner. She stood next to Jonas with confidence, and I realized I was now the one with a grimace on my face.

"Ladies and gentlemen, my beautiful daughter, Melissa. Maybe we'll have a double wedding?" Arthur mused, and the crowd clapped.

Jonas smiled at Arthur. He shook his hand, kissing Rita on the cheek.

"If you match my contributions and throw a party like tonight, I might consider it," Jonas said.

The crowd went wild.

My fingernails dug into my hands. Even though we were not together, I wasn't prepared to see Jonas move on. But this wasn't just him moving on. She was like Dani. A perfect match for him. I was happy when the lights dimmed, as I knew well enough I wouldn't able to hide the pain that gripped me.

Ian reached out and rubbed his hand on my arm, leaving a trail of warmth as well as an offer, if I was willing to take it. I wasn't. If I touched him I would fall apart. I was barely holding it together. Knowing Jonas was with her, and may have touched her like he touched me, hurt deeply.

Jonas launched into a speech about the Arthur Finch foundation and the list of charities with a video and power point presentation accompaniment. We were all spellbound as he went through the value that the charitable organizations brought to society like a true professional, inflicting the right intonation, and pausing at just the right moments. I was enthralled by his skill and proud of him at the same time.

Jonas paused as he reached the end of the list, his tone softening. "The final charity to make our list this year is an equally worthy addition. The Salomé Love Legacy."

The image that appeared next was of my parents and me at the first Perchance to Dream.

My jaw dropped open and I covered it with my hand. "How is this possible?" I spluttered.

"I don't know," Ian answered absently. "These things are usually set well ahead of time. Congratulations."

I then realized the picture had come from the Salomé Love Legacy's website. I had given Jonas the information weeks ago along with Ms. Parker's contact information. She would have had all my mother's binders, including a detailed diary with the progress of the event.

I was enraptured as Jonas continued his speech, speaking eloquently about the story I had shared with him about my parents. Tears flowed down my face in an endless stream to my heart.

He looked directly at me. "I will end with this special video that was created for tonight. Please enjoy."

The hall filled with an instrumental of *Adiago Cantabile* from Beethoven's, *Pathetique*. I didn't know where to go or what to do. He had completely undone me. My heart spilled over with love and gratitude as memories of our first night together came to mind. He had thought of me almost as too innocent that night, until he took possession of my body. We'd come together, and I knew even in those moments, and the subsequent days that followed, I was falling in love with him.

My shoulders shook and Ian lightly touched my back, alerting me that I needed to get a hold of myself. I gulped in air and dabbed my eyes with the facial cloths from my clutch. Then, I joined in on the applause that was deafening in the hall.

"If you would excuse me, I need to be alone for a few minutes. I'll be right back," I said quickly.

The lights were rising in the hall and I didn't want anyone to see my tear-streaked face or the overwhelming emotions that flooded me. Ian rose, but I turned and walked briskly away, not awaiting a response. I quickly maneuvered around the tables until I made it out of the hall. I walked outside, welcoming the cold air that cooled my skin. My mind was racing around all that I had seen this evening.

Finding a bench, I sunk down and tried to comprehend what had happened. Jonas helped fund my dream, my legacy.

"There you are."

I looked up to find Jonas charging toward me. My heart pounded in my chest as he stood before me, the electricity of our connection sparking between us and stealing my breath.

Jonas held out his hand for me to take. "It's too cold for you out here."

I clasped it and the spark of our connection came to life. A shiver went through me. Jonas didn't acknowledge it or pause. I found myself almost jogging beside him as he moved me back inside the building. Once there, he headed down a marble corridor away from the main hall and stopped before a room marked "Small Conference." He reached inside his inner pocket and removed a small card. He waved it before the door, releasing the lock, and closed it behind us.

I found nothing in the room that would be used in a conference. A small, fixed modular couch was set up along a corner, and there was a coffee table with snacks out for eating. Opposite that was a small buffet set-up and a kitchenette with a banner above it displaying, "Congratulations to Bryon and Rita on their upcoming wedding." Jonas lightly touched my waist and I turned around to face him. His gaze pinned me.

"I was completely off guard. I don't understand why you did it. But on behalf of my family and the program, thank you," I babbled.

"You don't have to say that," he said, still touching me.

"Yes, I do. I didn't. I mean I didn't set out to get your funding. I hope you know that," I stuttered.

"Take a deep breath," Jonas said, giving me one of his winning smiles.

He delighted in the effect he had on me. I stepped out of his arms and did as he asked. My breath eased, though my pulse still sprinted.

"As far as you seeking funding, that never came to mind. It was last minute that I was able to attend this gala, though your foundation inclusion was planned after we discussed it during our first evening together."

He paused and the memory washed over me, as well as a blush warming my face.

"I would have invited you, but you asked for space,"

Jonas said in a clipped tone.

I was happy he didn't mention our conversation on the phone or my ending our companionship. Reaching out, he took my hands in his. I peered up at him and looked down again. His presence was almost too much. I felt little next to him.

"But I'm trying to understand why you chose my project. There are so many other well established foundations that needed the money...."

"Why not? You told me about it. It seemed a worthy cause, so I had Finch add it to the list of charitable organizations this year. I spoke to Ms. Parker and she was on board with it. You said you were waiting for a promotion from Arch, but why should you wait when I can help you now?" Jonas said with a lift of his chin. "It's a start. The Finch Foundation will help connect your foundation with philanthropy committees, and the public. The Legacy can build on the exposure. Give you a start on your dream. You might one day head your family's foundation and not be just a publishing assistant at Arch."

In a flash, I realized what he meant. This was a stepping stone towards my dream of running the Legacy program and making it my full-time job. Jonas had made my dream into a possibility. I could keep the work and memory of my parents alive, and for his help with that alone, I was grateful.

"I can't express in words how much this means to me."

He said a lot of kind and supportive things. Still my mind niggled at his mentioning "just a publishing assistant." My greatest fear when it came to him was that I wasn't good enough. I needed to be better than I was to be any more than a companion to him. I swallowed down the sting, but his eyes were on me and rarely missed anything.

"Did I say something wrong? I hoped this would make you happy."

He pushed his hair back and a small smile formed on my lips. He had no idea how drop dead gorgeous he was. This wasn't the time, and I didn't have the relationship with him to discuss my insecurities.

"I am. Truly. I'm grateful," I said as fresh tears fell from my eyes.

Jonas cupped my face so that I was looking up at him. "You cry when you're happy?" he mused.

He guided me over to a small sink, where he dampened a cloth. He wiped clean the streaks on my face. His brows lowered and my pulse sped up as he scrutinized me.

"Dark circles. You're not sleeping." His gaze ran the length of me. "You've lost weight, too."

I peered at him through my lashes. "Are those compliments?" I tried to joke.

"No, but I'll give you one. You look beautiful tonight," Jonas said, his lips turned up in a smile.

My eyes connected with his, and when our connection sparked between us, my heart soared. I wanted him.

All of him. But he wasn't and couldn't be mine. I needed to leave.

"I should go…."

Jonas's eyes squinted. "I don't know why or how you got in touch with Ian. He didn't mention it when I saw him at the conference," he said hoarsely.

"With Melissa Finch." My voice rose at the end. I couldn't bring myself to look at him.

"Melissa had business in San Francisco, and she accompanied me. I wanted you to go, but you ended things with me," Jonas said.

I nodded, not trusting my voice. My gaze bore into him, willing him to define his plans with Melissa.

"Melissa and I are not together, but she was my companion before you." He cleared his throat.

I sat quietly hoping he would proclaim he wouldn't pursue more with her, but he didn't. He broke our silence by stating, "I didn't know you were dating Ian." His tone was clip.

"I'm not dating Ian. He invited me as a friend," I said.

"I know Ian, Lily, and friendship isn't his intention. I'm also sure he hasn't told you he wants to be only your friend," Jonas said.

I squirmed. "No. He didn't say that." I flicked my eyes at him and could see that seeing me with Ian bothered him. That wickedly made me feel better. "I still should go," I said, but didn't move from the spot in front of him.

Jonas held his hand out. "Can you spare a few more minutes with a friend?"

I looked up and his eyes softened as they bore into mine. I clasped his hand and let him guide me over to the small couch. I then watched as he unbuttoned his jacket and took the seat next to me. We stared at each other, unable to speak.

Could he feel the love I had for him?

Jonas moved closer and my pulse sped up. "You're hiding something and somehow I'm the only one that you're not sharing it with. That bothers me." His voice broke.

My face fell as shame filled me. I wanted to tell him, but I still worried I'd elicit his pity. I stared into his eyes, willing him to understand me. Once I was strong. I'd tell him everything.

"Maybe not tonight…." His finger stroking under my chin. "But I still want you to consider continuing our companionship."

I averted my eyes. "I told you how I feel. I feel like this is more."

I wanted more.

"Yes, but we haven't even been together long. And with my life what it is, I'm not ready for more," Jonas said softly.

My shoulders dropped. "It could be as it is now, but we could be truly dating…."

His eyes dulled, and he gave me a look as if I was a stranger. "The companionship works better for me. I'm barely divorced, and I'm a workaholic. I'm not ready for another committed relationship. What I can offer could be beneficial for both of us, if you'd let it be. Without the labels what is all that different?"

Tears filled my eyes. The difference being you would be mine completely and I'd have access to the heart he kept showing me. *You'd be mine.*

"I guess if you put it…."

"Lily. Don't."

Jonas cut me off with a kiss that stole my breath. He held out his hand again and I took it as he pulled me on his lap, his head bending down to nuzzle against my neck. He nipped me and a moan escaped my lips. My body heated up. His hand cupped the side of my face and turned my head so that I met his eyes.

"I can't sit here and not touch you. Not want you."

I wanted his touch, too, and moved to kiss him again. That was all he needed, and he responded by kissing over my face and down my neck. I found myself doing the same, kissing along the smooth-shaven skin along his square jawline. His mouth found mine and he kissed me hard, demanding access to my mouth. The familiar taste of Scotch and mints crossed my palette as his tongue tangled with mine. Jonas moved my back against the couch, and I panted as his hands pulled up the bottom of my dress, exposing the scrap of lace I wore beneath.

He sucked in a sharp breath as his gaze devoured me. "I prefer you bare, but I'll leave those on you," he said hoarsely.

My heart sung as I let out a shaky breath. Jonas had a way of making me feel desirable. My breasts swelled and I was slick between my thighs. Even though my mind admonished me for being so easy, I parted my thighs. There was nothing more I wanted at that moment than to feel his hands on me again. Jonas let out a triumphant groan as he slid a finger around the lace and the wetness there.

There was nothing more I wanted at that moment than to feel his hands on me again. Jonas let out a triumphant groan as he slid a finger around the lace and the wetness there.

"Soaking wet for me?" he asked roughly. "Open wider."

My breath hitched as a shiver went through me at his command. I followed his instructions and he rewarded me with sensual strokes through my pussy, rubbing the pad of his thumb around my clit while I moaned in pleasure.

He lifted his finger and traced my lips. "Did you let Ian taste you?"

He grunted. A peek at his jealousy; the same jealousy I had toward him with Melissa. My skin was on fire, but it cooled me on what was happening between us.

"You know I didn't. How could you ask that? You have Melissa," I said irritably.

"We haven't…." The unspoken "yet" hung in the air. He looked tormented. "I'm sorry, Lily. The thought of you with anyone…." Jonas went to his knees, and I peered down at him through a fan of lashes.

"I don't want anyone else touching you," I said, letting out a gasp as his fingers parted me, and his tongue languidly dragged through the slick flesh of my sex. I moaned again.

"Only me … So sweet," he whispered.

His tongue swirled around my swollen clit. The sight of this incredibly powerful leader on his knees, with his head buried between my thighs, was enough to send me over the edge. His fingers clutched my rear as he lapped and licked my pussy. The idea was heady and had me about ready to burst with the feeling of being desired and wanted. He pushed his tongue inside me and growled. My back arched as I ground my hips against his mouth, the pleasure consumed me. I was close to climax as his tongue lashed against me. I was unravelling.

"Come *for me*," Jonas grunted as he drew on my clit, and I did.

I shook with a full body tremor as the orgasm rippled through me.

"Jonas," I sobbed.

He wasn't done. He added another finger and stroked my inner walls as he gently suctioned my clit, demanding another climax. I loudly cried out as I quivered under him, forgetting where I was. Forgetting everything but him and his command over my body. As my vision cleared, and he allowed me to come down, he unzipped his trousers and pulled out his cock. I undulated, willing him to do what we both wanted. And he did, pushing in with one long thrust, filling me.

"Oh, God."

Oh, Jonas. Nothing like him. He took me with an urgency. Hard fast slams of his cock inside me, griping me tightly with his arms and gasping as he came.

"Come again," he gritted.

His jaw clenched tight as he moved his hand to stroke on my clit as he thrust into me. And I did, my legs convulsing around him as I gripped him tightly. We finally let go and he sat down on the couch next to me. I couldn't speak or move, but Jonas's words summed up everything.

"That's *my* Tiger Lily," he whispered.

I would have done just about anything he wanted at that moment. In pleasure, Jonas owned me. I was and wanted to be his. He leaned down and kissed me passionately, slipping his tongue inside my mouth and giving me a taste of my arousal. I gave myself completely to him and his kiss.

When we broke apart, Jonas nuzzled my neck. My hand was in his dark wavy hair.

"Don't you see what you're doing to me?" I whispered.

Before he answered, the door vibrated with a few succinct, hard raps.

"It's Melissa. Jonas? The TV stations are here. We need you now," she called out.

"I'll be right there."

Jonas cursed and stood, then moved to the sink and tried to clean up. I closed my eyes and pulled my dress down, ignoring the wetness soaking my thighs. How could I feel so incredible one minute and so dirty the next?

He touched my arm and held out a cloth. I took it and turned away.

"Just go, Jonas. You proved I can't resist you. You won."

He came around and wiped my thighs for me. There was something feral in his stare, as if he wanted to rub his scent all over my body, and stake a predatory claim on me. The more I thought on it, the more it thrilled me. The electricity between us flared as we stared at each other. In that moment, I had no doubt we were synced. We belonged to each other.

"There's no competition," he said bluntly.

The knocking started up again, and our moment broke apart. The reality of our situation set in. We weren't together.

"I said, I'm coming," Jonas barked out. His eyes glimmered and his voice softened. "We'll talk later."

He trashed the cloth and put back on his tuxedo jacket, moving to the door and unlocking it. Melissa filled the doorway and our eyes met. The disgust on her face amplified the shame on mine.

She curled her lips upward. "We're assembled in the gold room with club members. I'm sure your visitor here will understand and remain here. Well, this is Daddy's room. Perhaps she can—"

"Enough," Jonas said.

Melissa barred her teeth in what I supposed could be thought of as a smile. "Alright. I'm right outside."

She moved away from the door. Jonas also started moving away, only to turn at the gap.

"You can stay here," he said with authority.

I shook my head. "I'm leaving." I could tell from his facial expression that he was conflicted. "I'll be fine. Go."

He winked at me and turned away. I hunched my shoulders. Ian stepped up next to him outside in the hall. He looked past Jonas to me, and our eyes connected. All he needed to know was there. My skin flamed and I adjusted my dress.

Ian eyed Jonas coolly. "We'll talk later."

"Looking forward to it," Jonas said, strolling off with Melissa at his side without a backward glance.

I buried my face in my hands. Did he have sex with me out of rivalry or because he cared for me? If he cared, he wouldn't have been so adamant on re-establishing the boundaries of his companionship agreement. The sound of the door clicking closed stopped my thoughts cold. Ian was there, but I wasn't ready to face him. What was the etiquette for having sex with your ex on a date? This was a low, beyond anything I had thought possible of me.

"I'm sorry. I…."

"I don't blame you," Ian said. "I blame Jonas."

The couch dipped next to me.

"You should blame me. I didn't consider your feelings. I … We…."

I didn't know what to say.

Ian lightly tilted my head towards his and our eyes met. What I found on his face wasn't malice, which was a relief. But there was something else there that perplexed me. The look held an intimacy that we hadn't experienced together. My mind offered up numerous reasons he might have that look, but none I wanted to comprehend this evening. All I wanted was to be away from the gala and to be by myself to think.

My bottom lip quivered. "I'd like to go home, please."

Ian tucked my hair behind my ears. "Yes. I think that's for the best."

CHAPTER SEVEN

THE DARKNESS OF the night covered my guilt-ridden face. I sat static for the ride back to Jersey City. My borrowed dress, now stained and tucked close to my body, was low on my list of worries, though Natasha wouldn't think so. My thoughts were as blurry as the traffic speeding past the windows, but I was not so far gone that I didn't feel Ian staring at me. Ever the gentleman, he had insisted on seeing me home. He was honoring my silence, too, and that made it worse.

I knew Ian liked me, and that hadn't stopped me. No matter how I tried to pacify my conscience by telling myself I had attended this event with Ian as a friend; we were on a date—a fact even Jonas pointed out to me, but I had chosen to ignore. I behaved awful to a man that hadn't shown me anything but support and kindness.

When it came to Jonas, all reason left me. Being with him intimately felt right in my heart. I was without a doubt in love with him, but Jonas didn't feel the same way about me. He wanted me surely, but as a friend with benefits. He sexually reclaimed me after seeing me with

Ian. The more my mind went over this line of thought, the more I believed he'd taken advantage of me by being intimate with me, knowing my heart was at stake.

I gave in because I wanted him. My eyes stung in this realization. Ian reached over and clasped my hand. I looked at him, finding empathy and understanding reflected back at me.

He went even further by saying, "Your feelings are what I'm upset with Jonas about, not you having sex with him. You care deeply for him. You may even be in love with him. I know this, but he chooses not to see."

I let out a sob and Ian moved over in his seat and put his arm around me as I cried. I cried for Ian too. He was a good man and I had hurt him. Something was definitely wrong with me. He just whispered soothing words and stroked my back all the way back to Jersey City.

The car stopped moving and the door was ajar when Ian held out his hand to help me climb out.

My conscience attacked me again. Averting my eyes as I stepped onto the sidewalk, I said, "I apologize for behaving inappropriately as your date for this event. But I also want to apologize for causing problems between you and Jonas."

"We'll recover," Ian said as he walked me to the door of my building. "I'm more worried about you." He faced me. "I wasn't lying when I said what you did tonight didn't upset me. You're in love with Jonas—"

"I don't know … I don't know what to say," I said and rubbed my arms.

He smiled wistfully. "Okay. You don't deny it."

I couldn't. Not anymore.

We walked inside, and he rode the elevator with me up to my door. I turned to him in the doorway.

"Thank you, Ian. I'm sorry anyway. I don't want to lose you as … a friend."

He smiled. "You haven't lost my friendship. But think about tonight. And if I can be selfish for a minute, think about me. We have things in common, and in time we may find out a lot more about each other. I like you, Lily, and I'd like to see you."

I didn't understand why Ian still wanted me. He was right about our love of science fiction. He was kind and respectful regarding my issues with Declan. Still, I wasn't emotionally ready. I still wanted Jonas.

"I'm not past my feelings for Jonas. It wouldn't be fair to you."

Something else was bothering me and I met his eyes again. "Why aren't you upset about what I did with Jonas?"

Ian's gaze was pointed. "I don't think sex defines a relationship. I would have rather you didn't tonight, but I understand and as I said before I blame Jonas."

My lips parted. "It's not all his fault."

"I also understand why Jonas lost his head tonight at the idea of me touching you. Anyone touching you … You're special, Lily."

I gave him a confused look. Lost his head? I didn't see that, but Ian knew him better. My cheeks burned, too.

"Having sex in a small room in the middle of a fund-raising affair he was still working at isn't Jonas's style. Trust me. He lost his head," Ian said. His hand trailed down the side of my face. "So lovely," he said. "I'd love to get to know you better, Lily. It must be extraordinary to know you intimately."

I dropped my gaze from the darkness in the expression on his face, and I held in my breath. I didn't know how to answer, as what he was saying was well beyond where we had reached together. I didn't get a chance to ponder much more, though. Ian grabbed my hair tight and tilted my head back to him. He covered my lips with a kiss. He delved his tongue between my lips. Wow. He was going for broke. His kiss was skilled and demanding, and I found myself shockingly returning it.

What was I doing? I moved my head back and Ian let go, easing his hand from my hair, releasing me. I stood there, wide-eyed and panting, unable to say anything.

His eyes were dark as they gazed deeply into mine. "Thank you for that," he said softly. "That's a little taste of what you'd experience with me. I would give you time to heal, should you decide to move beyond Jonas. That's something I would never pressure you to do. I deal with things I see, and I told you what I believed true. Melissa's intentions are clear, but Jonas's, as you are aware, are not. I am, though. I'm here and available."

He didn't wait for an answer, just turned and walked away.

Ignoring the chiming of my phone, which was in my clutch bag that had slipped to the floor, I stared after Ian as he strolled down the hall to the elevator. When the doors opened, he turned back around to me. I felt a flutter go through me at the bright smile he gave. He touched his lips and disappeared as the doors closed.

I touched my own lips and closed my door as well. Why did I let him do that? Bending down, I opened my clutch and removed my phone. There was missed call and a text message from Jonas.

The interviews took a while and I'm sorry I didn't come back as quickly as I wanted to. I understand why you left. Call me back and we'll talk.

My heart leapt. I was ready to dial his number when I was interrupted by the sound of wailing. Natasha?

I ran down the hallway, past my room to her bedroom door. I had my hand on the knob and froze as my ears caught a lower toned yelp and the surprise music of … easy listening? I covered my mouth to suppress my laughter. Natasha had been my roommate for almost a year, and she had never brought someone back to visit, let alone stay over. She was too embarrassed of the décor and the fact that she wasn't living in Manhattan.

Natasha's boyfriend Ari making it inside the loft and her bedroom here was a huge step forward for her. Although, I knew their relationship was "complicated," as he was supposedly in the process of getting a divorce from his wife. According to Natasha, this process had been going on for over a year, but she told me she didn't mind. In fact, she often gloated about being the other woman, something I had looked my nose down at before I found myself in the weird status of being a semi-kept companion of Jonas. This status didn't sit well with me, but actually made her think better of me. A little.

Ridiculously tip-toeing away, I headed back to my door. I frowned as I pushed it open and found all the lights turned on in my room. Didn't I turn them off? A bit of annoyance gripped me. Natasha must have come in and left the lights on. Though, in all the months of knowing her, she had never done that before. She never had Ari over for a night, either. My eyes further scanned the room and I noticed the duvet was up on one side. Was she looking for an extra pillow? I used to put them there before we had agreed to put them in the hall closet. I exhaled long and let it go as I went about preparing for bed.

After cleaning up and changing for bed, I knew I put off long enough calling Jonas back. I quickly dialed his number.

"Hello?"

I recognized the voice and eyed the time. Melissa was answering his phone at midnight?

"Hi, Melissa. I'd like to speak to Jonas," I said.

"He's busy and we're going to bed," Melissa said.

My stomach lurched. We're? "Oh. Uh. Please let him know I returned his call," I replied vacantly.

"Do you think that's wise? I mean, you left and were all over his frenemy, Ian."

"Ian's not Jonas's friend?" I said, surprised.

"Jonas *thinks* they are, but he doesn't have many real friends. After tonight, I bet he won't have much to do with Ian. Most of his friends are business friends. People he has to work with professionally. Now he has the embarrassment of you muddying their relationship. I mean, seriously, what were you thinking?"

"I ... I." I had no words.

"Don't worry. I'll take care of him. Bring him back up after another betrayal. That's what I do. He used sex with you to cope and control everything around him."

It didn't feel that way. We both wanted and sought each other, or so I thought.

She continued, "It was a bit desperate, but I understand you have nothing and no one. Jonas told me as much, but I need you to help him now. Be a friend and stop trying to ruin all the progress he's made since Dani left him. Let him go, and give him the chance to find someone willing to not be so self-absorbed. Someone to be with him in the way he needs."

"I ... I didn't think," I stuttered over and over into the phone, which was now disengaged.

The sting of her words echoed through my brain and pureed my heart. I didn't even think of, or consider, how Jonas might feel about the mixed signals I gave to him. I did indeed break things off with him over the phone, then showed up at a dinner with his friend Ian, whom I had told him once I wasn't interested in.

I was self-absorbed and unwilling to compromise. After all, Jonas had shared the pain he experienced with his mother's illness, and his father's bitterness—how alone he was and his need to control the boundaries of his relationships to protect himself from the pain he experienced at the end of his marriage. Would I have preferred he lied, used, and dumped me?

I was alone in my love for him, but in a way Jonas was alone with me, too. He gave what he was willing to give, but without feelings. He wasn't hiding this from me, but I was hiding what happened to me from him.

I should leave him alone. He deserved, and could easily get, better than me—someone of his ... class.

My worry quickly went to self-loathing and caused bile to rise in my throat. I ran across the hall and emptied my stomach. I brushed my teeth, then numbly shook a couple of sleeping pills into my hands and took them.

CHAPTER EIGHT

M Y ALARM WENT off the next morning, pulling me from a deep and dreamless sleep. The fog of the sleeping pills clung to me, and when I opened my eyes, the sunlight through the glass of my floor to ceiling windows temporarily blinded me. I wiped my eyes a few times and rolled over towards the side of the bed closest to the window. I pulled my sluggish limbs to a standing position, making my way over to close the blinds. Last night's gala and Jonas came back to mind.

Last Night. I couldn't believe all that had happened last night. I had sex with Jonas, though we were supposed to be over. I kissed my new friend Ian back who probably heard me yell as I climaxed with Jonas on our date. My parents would roll over in their grave if they knew their daughter could behave so licentiously.

On the other hand, I didn't do anything I didn't want to do. Jonas was, and still remained, everything I wanted in my life. I wanted him on my terms, though. And as Melissa so willfully pointed out, I wasn't willing to compromise to keep him. Why won't I compromise?

Would giving myself to him be such a bad thing? Maybe in time he would grow attached to me. Maybe in time he would fall madly head over heels in love with me.

I puckered my brows as I tried to work this through in my head and make up my bed at the same time. Jonas wanted a mutual arrangement, though his actions were far from impersonal in his quest for intimacy. How could he possibly not see that or how much his actions affected me? And was I thinking about how my pushing him away affected him? Were we both too selfish?

I needed advice So, I decided to call Mary, who was overdue an update from me. I smoothed the duvet in place, then picked up my phone to call her. She answered on the third ring.

"Lily ... I'm." Her voice broke.

This woke me up out of my haze. "What's wrong?"

"Hans and I had a fight. I caught him with his skanky teaching assistant. I'm behind on all my papers and two are worth thirty-five percent of my term grade. If I fail, I can kiss my Ph.D. goodbye." She started sobbing.

I sat down on the bed. Hans and Mary had a some-what open relationship, which I knew Mary had taken advantage of in the past so I knew that wasn't actually what was upsetting her. Her academic career was what I knew to be the true source of her distress.

"What can I do to help?"

"Please, could you come to Somerville? I can't get my papers done." She gulped.

"Yes. Of course I'll come. I'll have to ask Gregor for a couple days off. We can do one of our old power sessions," I said as I walked over to my closet and pulled out a pair of denim jeans from my dresser. "I'll try to take a bus or train. So, seven to eight hours?" I bit my lip.

"Okay." She sniffed. "Would you bring your sociology research paper and syllabus from Dr. York's class with you? Oh, and bring your papers from history and anthropology. Maybe email them to yourself and we can take a look when you get here. Oh, just bring your laptop, but get the research syllabi for sure, please."

The corner of my mouth turned up. "Okay," I said, pulling one sleeve out of my t-shirt. "Anything else?"

"No. But I'll send you a text if I come up with anything else…." I could hear her sniffle. "I appreciate you coming out here. I know it's hard for you to be here, after…." The implication of my parents' death hung in the air, but went unmentioned. "I would have come down, but I have all this around me and I'm so upset. I…."

"Stop. Mary, you're my best friend. I'm there." I choked, my conscience bringing up Declan's recent attack. I had to tell her. "I need to talk to you, too."

"Oh. Something happen? I'm sorry for being so selfish. I didn't even ask," Mary replied.

I swallowed. "No, but yes … We'll have at least a few days to talk about everything."

"Okay. Give me a call or text the details. I can come and pick you up," Mary offered.

"Thanks, Mary. And don't worry. We'll get it all done and have time to watch a movie or two."

We laughed and hung up. I immediately dialed Gregor, but received his voicemail. I left a message requesting Monday and Tuesday off. Since I hadn't taken off time in a long while, I didn't think it would be too much, especially since he had offered a week off after he found out about my attack.

My stomach turned over as I thought about Declan, seeing him on the street, snarling at me. I started contemplating his lack of remorse, and that made me feel worse. I tried to push the thoughts aside and started packing for my trip to Boston.

Mary was right, I didn't like to return there anymore. The memories of my life with my parents, my family, were imprinted there. A walk down Newbury Street. Our nights at the Boston Conservatory for my father's performances with the orchestra. A shopping spree at Faneuil Hall sometimes came to mind. But what always overshadowed these visits was the ride down the main Highway 93, where their lives had ended.

I still remember the photo from the Boston Herald being handed to me by a neighbor "for safekeeping." It showed our black, four-door mangled vehicle with the Jaws of Life truck in the foreground, where they had removed their bodies from the wreckage. The neighbor had no idea, of course, how much I didn't want to see the wreckage or keep a copy of the article. One look imprinted the image on my mind, and challenged my will to live. One look had me transfixed before a mirror in my bathroom that night with a handful of sleeping pills, preparing to join them.

That didn't happen, only because Declan was there, pulling the pills away. He had stayed up all night talking to me, telling me how much my parents would have wanted me to live. That was the Declan I had fallen in love with, and wanted to marry. That was the Declan I knew was still buried in there. But I'd turned him in, my conscience chided. Yes. I had.

I exhaled and slid the closet door open, eying the designer trolley Jonas had bought me. *Jonas.* I grabbed my backpack and shoved in a couple pairs of jeans, jerseys, and underwear. I then crossed the hall to the bathroom and cleaned up, before picking up a few toiletries to take with me and returning to my bedroom. I dressed and brushed my hair into a ponytail. I pulled out a plastic tub from under my bed in search of old college papers. I noticed a few loose pictures of my parents were out of the album. My heart pulled as I put them back, then my phone buzzed. I answered with my free hand.

"Hello, Lily. It's Jonas."

I dropped my papers. "Oh. Hello."

"You didn't call back last night, and I don't blame you. I wanted to apologize," he said.

I licked my lips. "I left a message, but it was late. You don't need to apologize. We both did what we wanted to do."

"You left a message with … Melissa." I could hear

him putting the pieces together. "She stayed over in—"

"You don't need to explain anything to me," I interrupted. "I'll be fine. I'm fine."

"I don't believe you are. And from your tone, you're jumping to conclusions. I don't want to speak with you over the phone. I'll come and pick you up, and this time we'll talk. I promise."

I sifted through the papers and took out a few. "I can't. I'm heading to Boston to see Mary."

"When will you be back?" he asked.

"Not sure. Probably Tuesday," I said.

"I'll be leaving for Texas on Wednesday. Then away to London for another two weeks."

I blinked rapidly. "So you won't be around here for a while," I said in a small voice.

"That's my life, Lily. I work and travel. I try to get home when I can." He sighed. "How about I take you to Boston? I'm flying up to Connecticut today, but that won't take long. We'll ride the rest of the way from there."

"You don't need to go out of your way," I started, then stopped. "Wait. You're going to Connecticut to see your mother?"

"Yes. I need to settle some things there. Dani would normally go, but she's at a spiritual retreat with Alan this morning. I didn't have anything planned except taking Paul to the Knick's game at Madison Square Garden, and that's not until tonight."

A flutter went through my stomach. Jonas had told

me on one of our nights together that his mother suffered from early onset dementia, and that going with him to see her was one of the things Dani would do for him. It was just too hard for him to see her. His difficulty expressing his feelings wasn't limited to me.

My heart ached at the thought of him going alone. I wouldn't want to do that myself. "I'll go with you."

"Thank you. We'll be at your place to pick you up in half an hour?" he said. "Sorry such short notice, but with visiting hours…."

"I'll be ready. What should I wear?" I said before I caught myself.

"Want me to help dress you? I'll be right over," he teased.

I sucked in air. "No. I…."

"I was only kidding. Slacks and a shirt are fine," he said.

I then thought of Melissa. Why wasn't she going? "What about Melissa?"

"She'll be on our flight back to Texas on Wednesday," he admitted. "I didn't lie, I'm not with her."

We were silent for what felt like a minute, but it was probably only a few seconds.

"Alright. See you soon."

I put the phone down. My mind wanted to dissect the conversation, but I didn't have time.

On my third pass through my papers, I found everything I thought Mary would need. I ended up having to use the trolley, as I needed my laptop, too. So I quickly repacked my clothing and changed into a pair of black wool pants and a grey button down shirt. I even managed a smear of gloss on my lips before the door sounded. I pulled out my phone and sent a quick text to Jonas.

I'm walking out of my apartment and will meet you outside

This was not a date, I told myself, as I quickly grabbed my handbag and keys before walking out the door.

My pulse sped up at the sight of Jonas standing outside of the apartment building waiting for me. His gaze connected with mine, and the tension charged the air between us. A shiver went through me, as my eyes zoned in on the smile curving his full lips. I couldn't help but acknowledge the effect he had on me. He was stunning, in a dark turtleneck and grey slacks. I laughed internally, thinking how we matched. His brow rose questioningly as I approached.

"You look beautiful."

They were words he often said to me, that magically relaxed me. A little boost to my confidence that he somehow understood I needed. It was one of the many things that had my heart skipping a beat when I was with him.

He leaned down and brushed my cheek, then took my bags and handed them to David, who walked over to collect them. I smiled at our driver shyly, a blush appearing on my cheeks. After having loud and passionate sex in the car with Jonas, my embarrassment had become a part of our greeting.

A chilly gust of wind came past and I shuddered, which in turn had Jonas reaching for my hand and walking us over to the car. As I looked down at my ankle boots, I noticed the dusting of snow on the sidewalk. Winter wasn't exactly over, but New York City didn't usually get this cold. Not as cold as Boston, for which I now realized I had under-packed. Nevertheless, I climbed inside the car and took off my coat, passing it through to place in the trunk.

Jonas climbed in and settled next to me. I turned to him and noticed a tightness around his eyes, and a slight turn down to his mouth. He tried to cover both once our eyes met. This was difficult for him. I reached out and took his hand, clasping it.

David pulled off and drove down the street, the crush of the dusting of fresh snow under the tires. The sun was beaming down. If the temperature hadn't been so cold, it would have melted the snow by now.

"I'm sorry about leaving you last night. As part of the press for the foundation, we have to do some interviews. I understand why you left with Ian."

The words were weighted as if he wanted to ask more about what happened between myself and Ian last night.

I licked my lips. "I didn't mean to come between your and Ian's friendship or business relationship. One kiss is all I had with him. He was helping with some legal stuff—"

"What legal stuff?" Jonas interjected.

I chewed my lip. "The thing I'm not yet ready to discuss with you, but will when I feel better." I dipped my head down. "Please don't push it," I said in a small voice.

"I won't, but I want to know. I can help if you'd give me a chance," Jonas said. He lifted his arm. "Can I hold you?"

He read my need for comfort and asked. He didn't take or order. There was the difference. I was no longer his companion. I moved over and placed my head on his chest, and the warmth and comfort filled me. I could have wept.

My mind played over what he had shared about his mother in the past. He once told me she had placed him in boarding school early and left his father for his friend. Not exactly great childhood memories. And now, his mother didn't seem to remember any of it, conflicting his feelings even further. To what extent, I didn't know. His pain was evident in his telling and had led me not to press him for an answer at the time.

"So, how about those Knicks?" I asked to break the tension.

He laughed and I joined him.

"Paul is looking forward to that this evening." He squeezed me. "We should talk about us, but later. If that's alright?"

There was a sadness there that caused a tightening in my chest. "Sure. So, will your younger brother, Vincent, be there?" I asked, changing the subject.

From Jonas's expression, this topic wasn't one he was ready to discuss either.

"Don't know." Jonas stared out the window. "I didn't call to tell him."

"You're fighting?" I asked.

He shook his head. "Nope. Vincent feels he does everything and I don't do enough, though he wouldn't dream of opening his wallet to pay for the five-star resort he insisted on placing mom in. They visit every other Sunday and I visit when I can, and that sums up our normal relationship. He's perfect, and I'm a shit." He swallowed.

I grimaced. "I don't believe that's true. Is there another place you want her to be?"

He ran his tongue over his bottom lip. "It's not about the money. It's his attitude and the expectation that goes along with it. He acts as if I owe him. He's like my father—nothing was ever enough for them."

I pursed my lips. "I'm sorry, Jonas, but he's wrong. If he treats you like that, you don't deserve it, not with all the hard work you do for your family, staff, and companies. You're not selfish."

"I'm not perfect, Lily," Jonas said. "I feel better, though, so thank you." He moved over and pressed his lips against my forehead. "Dani mentioned she hugged you recently and it warmed her heart so much that she cried all the way back home."

A tightness formed in my chest. She had cried for

what happened to me. I couldn't bring myself to tell him that, though, so I just dropped my head and nodded.

"I told you about Dani to let you know that talking to you warms me too. I feel better, just being with you," Jonas said, as if he had to offer me an explanation. "I need one of your hugs right now, too."

I allowed him to position me across his lap, and wrap his arms around me. I closed my eyes and inhaled, taking in his scent, which I found intoxicating and comforting. Whatever we were to each other at the moment didn't matter. We took comfort in each other's arms the rest of the short drive to Newark Airport.

CHAPTER NINE

T HE THIRTY-MINUTE FLIGHT got us to Hartford just before noon. During the short wait to board the plane, I texted Mary and informed her of my detour, which would actually be getting me to her sooner than I had originally promised. I also provided added assurance that I had brought my laptop and would be poised and ready to start a marathon session of studies once I arrived in Boston.

Jonas had arranged a car, which David went to collect once we arrived at the airport. We rode silently up the long stretch of highway toward Windsor, Connecticut and turned off into one of the suburban upscale neighborhoods before driving through a stone and iron gate marked Henning Estates. As I took in the surroundings, I thought Jonas hadn't exaggerated when he said the nursing home appeared more like a resort. Although it was covered in snow, even that looked manicured. Everything was perfectly in its place, from the gazebos to the low bridge streams.

We parked in front of what I would consider a brick

and stone mansion, boasting Doric columns with marble footings. A ramp rose conservatively along the side, well blended in along the long porch, which was partially insulated where a few people were seated. They appeared to be listening to a woman in a uniform read aloud to them. Jonas opened the door, and a little chime went off announcing our entrance.

The inside was befitting the exterior; upscale décor with crystal chandeliers, and toned floral patterned plush seating. There was a large fireplace and a grand piano in the living area. Amidst the affluence was some cleverly placed signage as well as a nurse's station. The pungent scent of disinfectant cleaners made it clear this may be a home to some, but it was also a business. A few residents were seated, their eyes fixed on us as we stood there. One middle-aged female in uniform came from behind the nurse's station and approached us with an open smile.

"I'm Brenda. Family Relations Manager. May I help you?" Her smile deepened in recognition. "Sorry, Mr. Crane. Your mother Joselyn should be back from the Crane Institute by now. If you don't mind waiting a minute, I'll go check and escort you up to her suite."

Jonas nodded, and she rushed off.

I touched his arm. "I could wait for you down here if you would prefer to see your mother alone."

His eyes clouded over. "That won't be necessary. This won't take long."

I frowned, and was about to ask him what he meant, when Brenda came back. "She's available, and we can use an office there for the papers I need you to sign, as we discussed. If you'd follow me."

"How is she?" he asked, as we walked over to a wall that turned out to be a well-hidden elevator.

Brenda pressed the top floor then glanced at me. Jonas simply nodded.

"She's doing fine," Brenda said. "Blood pressure is under control. We will continue to monitor her adjustment to the new medication. Otherwise, everything is pretty much the same."

"That's good," Jonas muttered.

The doors opened and we all climbed out. Brenda waved a pass and we entered a plush, neutrally toned suite.

"Would you like to go over the paperwork? I can have Miss...." Her eyes turned to me.

"Lily," Jonas said. "Apologies to the both of you. Yes, Brenda, we can go over the paperwork now. Lily can ... meet Joselyn. I'll join her once we're done."

Brenda nodded slowly, then held out her arm for me to follow her. I noticed similar décor to the downstairs, with a few personal photos thrown in. I immediately recognized Jonas and Mathias, as they were very much in the public eye. Dani and Paul were represented as well. My eyes stopped on a shorter man who appeared in a few photos. He had reddish-blonde locks and large brown eyes that stared out of some of the pictures with a young, handsome Jonas. Vincent? I pondered.

I didn't have long as Brenda motioned for me to take

a seat in one of the loveseats before a flat screen television. I inhaled the aroma of Chanel No. 5 fused with the velvety soft fabric. The smell, along with the beautiful bouquets of lilies, tactfully hid the sanitized scent. I stared at the lilies for a moment in admiration.

"Aren't they beautiful?" Brenda asked. "Jonas has them delivered every few days. Joselyn loves lilies. They were her wedding flower. Well, her first wedding," she added the last words in a hushed tone. "Mr. Crane definitely spoils her. Everything and anything she can remember, he gets for her. And we put it all around her room. You know, to trigger her memory. But there is no cure."

We both went quiet.

"Yes. That must be really hard for Jonas and her family," I said.

"Well, she's luckier than most. Some don't get visits, just money. Her son Vincent comes see her every Sunday," she said. "Jonas comes too when he can," she quickly added along with a smile.

"Jonas travels and works," I said.

She nodded in agreement, then turned the television on and a soap opera I recalled from my days of watching them in my teens flared to life.

"I'll be right back," she said.

She walked out of the room and returned a few seconds later with a tall, curvy female. The woman was dressed casually in a cream cashmere turtleneck and beige wool pants, but made both appear rich and elegant. Her reddish blonde hair was brushed back in a tight chignon, showing off a beautiful pair of pearl earrings along with the sculpted plains of her face. She was striking, even with the creases around her pale blue, vacant eyes. A small smile appeared on her bow lips on approach.

"Hello…."

She paused. There was a slight tremor to her stance.

"This is Lily. A friend of your son, Jonas. You haven't met her before," Brenda said.

Her brows puckered. "I don't have any children. You're mistaken…."

Her eyes fixed on Brenda for a clue or correction.

"Yes. You do you have two sons, Jonas and Vincent," Brenda said in a playful tone.

"Oh. Yes," Joselyn said, but she didn't appear convinced. Her gaze shifted back to me. "I do think I know her, though." I stood and awkwardly shook her hand, which she took in a loose shake as she assessed me. "Whose family did you say you were?"

She looked down her nose at me.

"I … I didn't," I stuttered.

"She's Lily. Your son Jonas's friend," Brenda said, furthering her correction on Jocelyn's claim that she had no children. "Remember Jonas?"

She went and picked up a picture, one that displayed a young Jonas in uniform.

"Jonas," Joselyn repeated.

She looked at me as if she was poised in wait for my confirmation.

I swallowed hard. "Yes. Jonas. He's handsome in that photo. Your son."

"Mathias's son," she muttered. "I did my part."

I touched my lips and Brenda quickly took the photo away. "I'll be right back."

She turned the volume of the television up and left the room. I shifted in my seat and we watched the television in silence. I stole glimpses of Joselyn, and the door, pondering what I should do until Jonas returned.

"Who are you, Miss?" Joselyn asked.

I turned to her and from her expression it was as if our short time together had been erased and we were being introduced.

"Lily. Lily Salomé," I said and cleared my throat. "I'm a friend of your son, Jonas."

She stared off and then turned back to me with a beaming smile.

"Lily. Oh, yes. Lily. You're beautiful."

Her smile slipped off her face as the door opened, and in walked Jonas and Brenda. He had his air of authority, but there was also something guarded.

His eyes shone. "Hello, Mom. It's Jonas."

My heart constricted as I found his voice so similar to that of a child.

Her face contorted into a snarl. "Get the hell out of here, Mathias," she gritted. "I don't want you here. I don't want to ever see you again. I told you, I don't love you. I'm in love with Shaun. We're leaving you and *your* son."

My heart tumbled to the floor as I looked at Jonas. His head fell forward. I rushed over and grabbed his hand. I tugged his arm as Brenda eased over to Joselyn, blocking her view of Jonas, as she attempted to soothe her.

"Now, Joselyn. You know that's not Mathias. That's your son, Jonas."

"Tell Shaun he came back here," she demanded. "Go back to your whores. Don't come back here," she yelled out.

Once we were outside his mother's suite, I wrapped my arms tightly around his waist and rubbed his back.

"I'm fine," Jonas assured me on his third try. I didn't listen, just held on. "She doesn't know what she's saying."

He pressed his head against mine, and my heart wept for him.

"Oh, the prodigal son decides to come by."

I turned and saw the older version of the young reddish-brown haired boy from the photos. His face had the similar handsome, chiseled structure to Jonas's, but that was where the similarities ended. His navy suit was tailored, though he was stocky and at least a foot shorter than Jonas, whom I thought was at least six foot one. His eyes, which were similar in color to his mother's brown eyes, were squinting at us. His mouth twisted in a grimace.

"My brother, Vincent," Jonas announced. He released me and straightened. "We are finished with our visit."

"Can't handle a little bit of reality?" Vincent asked.

Jonas started moving us past him when he grabbed his arm.

"Run away and leave the real work behind. Leave your poor, sick mother," Vincent sneered.

"Release him," I hissed.

His anger shifted to me, but he let Jonas go, and stepped back.

"She was cruel to him, and hysterical," I said. "He had to leave so she would calm down."

"She wouldn't be that way if he came around more often," Vincent started up again. "Instead, he avoids her all the time—"

"I don't recall Jonas mentioning your extensive study in dementia. You're a doctor? Scientist? I didn't know you studied brain chemistry. Or are you some kind of healer? Give us a cure, you self-righteous jerk," I said between clenched teeth.

Vincent's eyes widened and he stood there stunned for a few seconds as his hand slipped off Jonas. His face reddened.

"Who the hell are you to tell me…?"

I jutted my chin. "I just did."

I turned to Jonas and his mouth opened. "This is Lily."

I held out my hand and he took it, though I think we both knew there was nothing pleasant about this shake. We then walked over to the elevator and I pressed the button.

"We're leaving," I said.

Once we were inside, I deflated. I didn't know what had come over me. I just couldn't stand by and watch him crush Jonas's spirit. All I knew was that I wanted to stop his pain.

My cheeks warmed in embarrassment. "I'm sorry. I don't know what had come over me."

A ghost of a smile appeared on his lips. "That was the best visit I've had in years. Thank you, little tiger. Or should I say lioness?"

I smirked, but didn't say anything. He was right. I did feel extra protective of him. He tucked me against his side and we walked together out of the building, my thoughts as certain as my heart. Jonas Crane belonged to me.

"Is she always like that, Jonas?" I asked.

He blinked. "No. At times she thinks I'm Mathias and we just married. Other times, she doesn't remember anyone."

I wrapped my arm around his waist and we walked together, outside to the car that was parked out front. Once we got inside, Jonas sat still. An uneasiness settled between us. I didn't understand how I could feel so close one minute and so far away in the next. I was unclear what had changed, but as the minutes went on, my stomach soured. As were my thoughts.

"We should have lunch before we go to your friend's home," Jonas said. "How about Thai? There is a nice

Thai restaurant nearby."

I licked my lips. "I want to talk about something. Our companionship. I'd like to try again," I blurted.

His eyes glimmered and he interlaced his fingers with mine. "I don't think that's possible, not with how we feel about each other. I have feelings for you, but I'm not ready for more. My life is my work and family. I travel and I can only do short stays in New York. With my book being published, possibly next year, I have a lot more promotional engagements, which will take me away even longer."

"I understand that," I said. "We discussed as much before. I didn't mean to put a demand on your time. I had too many expectations. We have only been together a short while. I didn't realize that until now. I want to try and compromise."

"You shouldn't have to compromise. I was being selfish when I can see so clearly that you…."

He let the words die, but we both knew what he was having a hard time saying. I knew in my heart that I had fallen in love with him. I had formed an attachment in a way that blossomed out of our intimacy and moved on to wanting a more secure commitment, something he wasn't ready or willing to give me. I stared at him, and saw his struggle. As well as the resolve. He was letting me go. My mouth went dry as my face jumped, unable to settle as everything fell apart.

"I wasn't sure until now. I regret hurting you. It was something I was concerned about from the beginning, but I was too selfish to not have taken you for myself. I'm too much like my father."

Jonas's hands trembled as he collected a cloth and started wiping my face.

My lip quivered. "You're nothing like your father."

Not from what he had shared, what I'd read about him, or even what his mother said in the nursing home.

When I continued, my voice was just above a whisper. "Let me try."

But looking at him, I knew that wasn't going to happen.

"Try not to care?" Jonas said softly. "Impossible. Your heart isn't made that way. I'm selfish. I'm used to things going my way in my life. I oversee all that happens and control its flow. That's how I survived and made things work for me. Relationships have to fit into what I have to give and that's not what you need. I want to do the right thing for you."

I swallowed hard, unable to answer. My mind played over what Melissa had warned me of before. Jonas had needs, too. Needs that outweighed what I wanted from him. Being with me would only make him feel out of control and lost again. I needed to get myself together.

"I don't want you out of my life, and friendship is better for us right now," Jonas said to me, and himself, I supposed.

I shook. My mind reached out and held on to "right now" for a sliver of hope to wrap up my heart that was breaking apart. I didn't care about my tears. I didn't want to care about anything.

"Lily, please," Jonas pleaded. "Don't cry. I'm not going anywhere. I'm still your friend, and I will be that forever. Whenever you need me, I'm here."

He kissed my lips again and again and I let him, tasting the saltiness of my tears as he tried to coax me to calm.

"Try for our friendship," he said. "Promise me."

"I promise," I was incoherent.

Even though I promised, I didn't see the possibility. I loved him. Couldn't he see that? Didn't he care? What-ifs played through my mind as this incredible man I loved was moving out of my life. What-if I had agreed last night, would we be making love right now? *Making love.* I loved him and wanted his love back.

"We are pulling up to the Thai restaurant," Jonas said.

I shook my head. "I'll eat at Mary's. Please, I just want to go now."

Jonas gave me a look as if he wanted to argue, but he didn't. That was when I knew for certain that he had already left me.

We made it to Mary's in record time. Part of me thought David must have sensed the urgency and drove like the Devil was behind him down the highway until he reached her apartment in Somerville. I pulled out my phone to text her once we reached her street so that she would meet me at the gate. The three-story Victorian house was a bit of a commute for Mary to Boston

College, but it was less expensive than living in Chestnut Hill, though she had to make extra time to drive and park for her burgeoning course schedule. While plowed, the snow was heavier in Massachusetts.

Our silence was tense. There wasn't anything left to say between us. Jonas had let me go, and the more we stayed in each other's company, the harder it would be. I wanted to argue and state a case against his decision, but I realized that wasn't fair to him. I wasn't enough for him. I had thought as much myself.

As the car pulled up, the front door of the house opened and out came Mary. I smiled despite everything. Mary was in her "no-fuss-academic crunch attire" that consisted of a red tank top a few shades lighter than her hair, which was all atop her head in a messy ponytail. Her flannel pajama bottoms were red with cows all over them. She had on her cow slippers so she matched, I thought in amusement. Her horn-rimmed glasses covered her pale green eyes that I was willing to bet were squinting.

I climbed out and she came down the stairs, her lush mouth agape, but she quickly recovered and jutted her pointy chin. No sign of distress, as I suspected. She bounded down to us, her arms wide. I closed the distance and gave her a hug.

"Good lord, Lily. Are you eating?" she griped.

I hugged her back. "Plenty."

We broke away and she held her hand out to Jonas, who took it with one of his winning smiles that worked one out of her, too.

"Mr. Jonas Crane," Mary said. "Nice to meet you. Would you care to come in for some homemade pizza?"

"Nice to meet you, Mary. I wish I could, but I will have to decline. I need to get back to New York," Jonas said.

She looked between us, and slowly nodded.

"Okay. I'll just take your bags, Lily, and look through them for the papers. Nice to meet you too, Jonas," Mary said, walking over to David to collect my bags.

When she moved back up to the house, I turned back to Jonas. My heart constricted at the troubled look on his face.

"I'm still here. I'll always be here for you. Call me and let me know how you are and I'll do the same," Jonas said.

I gave a quick nod, not necessarily trusting my voice, and sucked in air.

"Would you give me a smile I can take with me?" he asked, his eyes watery.

I swallowed hard and smiled through the tears stinging my eyes again. He wiped my cheeks. The thought of never seeing him again weighed heavily on me, and I felt sure this might be my only chance to tell him my feelings.

"I love you, Jonas."

My voice sang out, and hung in the air. I squeezed him tight, then ran up to the house, not stopping to look behind me.

CHAPTER TEN

I CLOSED THE door behind me and rested my back against it. I longed to settle my heart, which was trying to escape my ribcage. I told Jonas Crane that I loved him, after he told me he was letting me go. Pain seared my chest at the thought of being let go right when I was ready to compromise. Jonas said he didn't want to hurt me, but it was too late. I was crushed.

My conscience decided to berate me for my cowardice in running off after telling him. But what would I have faced if I remained? He had ended things between us, so all he had to offer was not saying he loved me back. That, and a dose of pity, neither of which my heart was ready to face.

Therefore, I decided my telling him was an act of bravery. Or so I assured myself as I turned to peek through the small row of glass windows running the length of the doorframe, looking to see if the car was still there. *No.* It was gone and so was Jonas. Tears stung my eyes as I crumbled to the floor. Once again, I was heartbroken. Once again, I wasn't enough for the man I loved.

"Oh, Lily." Mary was suddenly in front of me, sinking down on the floor next to me. "What did your gorgeous businessman do? You both looked like lost puppies."

My sob turned into a laugh, but began crying again. This prompted her to quickly dash for tissues to help mop me up. When I really gave myself to crying, it wasn't pretty. I was a blotchy-faced, nose-running, mouth-dripping nightmare. With this amount of crying, Mary understood the cause. She recalled a similar collapse when she came to visit me after Declan had dumped me. So she waited there patiently for me to empty myself out, offering sympathetic words and a few pats and rubs on my back. Once I had passed the hiccupping stage, I was ready to share my woes with her. Never mind that I was technically here to help with *her* problems.

I really was self-absorbed. Before my mind could take over the self-loathing tape, I launched into a brief synopsis of my romantic life.

Jonas broke-up with me, though we weren't really seeing each other," I said hoarsely. "He had an epiphany that came to him after we had mind blowing sex yesterday, he decided that I had become too attached to him, and he wasn't ready for more. He took me to visit his mother in the nursing home, which was just heartbreaking. Then…."

I gulped in air. Mary let me collect myself again and

I continued. "He gave me the 'I don't want to stand in the way of your happiness' speech," I said, surprising myself at how far into bitterness I had reached. But with Mary's "you go girl" scowl on her face, I went further into that space. "He won't stand in the way, just so long as my happiness isn't derived from dating his friend Ian, who I kissed last night on our date at a gala event."

Mary looked befuddled and I realized I was rambling now, so I decided to skip our conversation to the bottom line. "I got too clingy, just as you warned me. I went against our agreement and fell in love with him. I couldn't help myself. When I'm with him, it's the most intense connection I have ever experienced. It's intimate, romantic. He's demanding, but so loving. I love him. I just told him so...."

I was back to lovey-dovey, and that got me an empathic look from Mary.

"I said those things to you because he's only the second guy you've ever been with. You spent such a short period of time together, and he told you upfront he wanted a casual, sexual friendship. I just ... I wasn't sure you would ever be up for that. And I think you knew that all along, as well," Mary said bluntly.

My mouth opened and closed. I didn't want to argue. That was Mary, no nonsense when she decided there were logical conclusions available to offer insight into a situation. Perhaps I needed a dose of reality.

She stood up and offered her hand. I clasped it and she tugged me to my feet.

"Let's talk more over lunch," Mary said.

She moved away from me and made a jaunt toward her small kitchen to attend to what my nose had deduced was a burning homemade pizza.

I removed my shoes and looked around where I stood. The space was small, as most converted Victorian homes in this area of Boston were, with a combination living room and dining area. It had the pretty fireplace, some of the original crown molding, and elegant light fixtures, but that was where the charm ended. Four tall bookcases dominated the space, packed with books and enough kitsch to make a grandma raise a brow, or so I imagined. Being the only living relative of both my parents' lines left me with only TV shows as a reference. Her small, old-fashioned twenty-inch TV was on, playing what I thought to be a documentary, though the volume was turned down. I supposed it was part of her studying by osmosis. The small fabric couch, chair, and rug, were littered with more books and papers. Her dining area was no less cluttered. She had it set up like an office with a desktop computer, printer, and papers stacked and organized on top of her small, round table. It all reminded me that Mary was in term paper mode and I would be put to work soon.

I rolled and parked my trolley bag at the end of the table, then joined Mary in the small alcove that was her kitchen.

"You're worse than Gregor," I teased as I took a seat at the small table there.

"Am not," she retorted, passing me a bottle of wine. "He's a disaster. How is he?"

I rose to open the wine as she set two slices of pizza on each of our plates. I quickly filled her in, telling her about the kiss as well.

"Told you he's crazy about you," she said smugly.

I rolled my eyes. "He's not. He was just confused at the time."

"Because you don't like him. That's the only reason you're saying that," she said adjusting her glasses.

I didn't respond, as it hit too close to Jonas and myself.

Mary quickly changed the subject. "Life moves too fast up there. I'm kind of happy I'm over here."

She sat down with the plates.

"I'm sorry I dumped this all on you. Tell me what happened with you and Hans," I said, taking a bite of my pizza.

"Fine," Mary said, lifting her chin. "Hans and I had a fight because he had sex with his teaching assistant. And before you point out that I agreed to an open relationship, we also had a few rules in place. We were to be open and honest about it. He had sex with her once, which we agreed to. Then I learned they were fucking every afternoon thereafter. I think he has feelings for her, so he's going to explore that."

She bit into her pizza as I gaped at her. She was almost frosty now, not anything like she had been on the phone.

"After two years?" I asked, my voice raising. "That's it? Aren't you upset?"

"I am. I was. I cried already. Eat," she said as she sipped her wine. "Crying won't change anything. I'm focusing on what I have control over right now. And that's my studies and career, which we will get to after you tell me the rest. I don't feel like talking about it anymore right now ... So, spill it woman."

I reached over and squeezed her hand, and she drained her glass of wine, the only sign that she was still upset. I knew from experience that if I pushed her, she would get snippy. I respected her wishes and filled her in between bites of the abysmal pizza made with some odd flavorless cheese. I told her everything I had left out earlier between Ian and Jonas, omitting Declan from all of it. I just wasn't ready for that conversation yet.

"I risked carbs for this," I said at the end, taking my last bite of pizza. "Yuck."

Mary giggled. "It's not that bad, and you're not eating." She adjusted her horn-rimmed glasses and made sure I caught her glare. "Something else is going on with you, but first ... *Meow.* What a hot little cat you are, two guys! I'm impressed. Ian sounds hot, but don't be that girl that goes through a guy's friends. I love you like a sister, but that's skank territory."

My cheeks burned. "Thanks, Mare."

"I'm only saying these things because I adore you my beautiful, dorky friend," Mary said and beamed at me. "As for me, I'd give Ian a go. Who did he look like again?"

I laughed. "Kind of a Rosenberg, a bit of a Hemsworth. I don't know … hot."

She wagged her brows. "Geeky, too? I might be in lust. I'll need to make a trip up to New York soon."

I laughed, but she actually looked serious. Whether she wanted to admit it or not though, she loved Hans.

"What about Hans?"

"I don't know. Maybe I need a sex-esteem boost. Since he's so busy with his assistant," she grumbled.

I squeezed her shoulders. "Think about it first. It's too fresh to make any hasty decisions."

The sound of my phone chiming made my heart skip a beat as I pulled it out to answer. Mary's face lit up, but turned concerned when she saw the corners of my mouth turn down.

Number unrecognized.

"Not Jonas," I mumbled. "Hello?"

"Hello, is this Ms. Lily Salomé?"

"Yes," I replied.

"I'm Diane Langston of Langston, Harrison, and Fitzpatrick. Ian sent me your information to follow up on a possible criminal and civil filing against Declan Gilroy. Now, he was arrested a few days—"

"Arrested?" My jaw unhinged. "Oh, my God. I didn't think. Uhm…." I looked over at Mary and saw her brows rise questioningly. I waved my hand and walked towards the front door, as I tried to settle the jolt to my heart. "I didn't agree to that."

"It's a police matter and part of procedure. I'm sure you were aware of that, though it usually doesn't happen this quickly. But then again, you had Ian Unger's assistance. Now, as for the civil case matter—"

"I don't want to sue him. I really just want this all to go away." I lowered my voice. "I want to put this behind me. I'm sorry, but I'm not available to discuss this right now."

"Well, when will you be? I can make an appointment for you next week."

I could hear the sound of her shuffling papers around, as well as Mary walking up behind me.

"I'll call you back. Okay?" I said quickly.

"Okay."

She drew out that last word before ending the call.

I knew Mary had heard enough and wasn't going to drop this. I had run out of time. Putting my phone back in my pocket, I met Mary's questioning stare. My mind conjured up memories of our lengthy friendship. She had always been a good friend to me, and what had I done but keep secrets from her? I rubbed my souring stomach.

"I got a restraining order against Declan. He ... beat me."

The shock and dismay on her face made me want to turn away, but she deserved the whole truth.

"He had been hurting me physically, off and on, for the past two years. You already know how snarky he could be from the times you met him, but that was the least of his cruelty. He said things that hurt me so much." My voice went monotone. "You know I hadn't seen him for months, but I met with him over lunch, and he hit me. Declan promised he would get help this time. But he didn't. Instead, he showed up at my job and scared me. Dani found out, and she and Ian helped me to get a restraining order so he would leave me alone."

Mary did a great impression of a fish out of water for a few minutes. I stood, holding my waist, and waited.

"That fucking asshole hit you! I knew he was a scumbag, but I didn't realize … How could I not know? How could this happen?" Mary's anger boiled over. She shoved over a stack of books before turning back to me. "Why didn't you tell me?"

The hurt look on her face was more than I could take, and I dropped my head. She pulled me into crushing hug as she broke down in tears. The guilt, shame, and sorrow over hurting her had me crying again, too.

"I'm sorry, Mary," I hiccupped. "I loved him. I didn't want to give up on him. You know what a hard life he had. He was abused and abandoned. I thought he needed love and family. I wanted to give him all that," I tried to explain as I wiped my eyes with the back of my hand. I forced myself to meet the devastated look on her face. "You hated him so much, I was afraid you would think less of me for staying. I … I wanted it to be my decision to leave him. But, well, he ended up leaving me. I'm sorry," I sobbed.

"I'm sorry too, Lily," Mary said, wiping her eyes and

picking up her discarded glasses. "I didn't realize I made you afraid to tell me the truth. You're right. I would have worked to my last breath to make that prick suffer and forbidden you to speak to him." Her eyes widened. "I mean, if your dad and mom knew…."

Mary knew how close I had been with my parents. Seeing their disappointment reflected in her eyes ripped apart my heart.

"If they knew," she continued, "you kept this from them. They would have been devastated. This would have broken their hearts. How could you keep that from them, from us? We are supposed to be your family."

She covered her mouth.

Her words broke me. The self-hatred filling me was unlike anything I had ever felt before. Bile rose up in my throat and I took off for her bathroom. Barely making it, I threw up violently into the toilet, which was surprisingly relieving. I continued dry heaving over the basin until my throat was raw and my stomach muscles ached too much to continue. Part of me wished I was back in New York and alone. I had known it would be hard to tell her; however, thinking of how much I would have hurt my parents was almost more pain than I could bear. They would have discovered how weak I am, not the brave daughter they brought up.

I did what worked for all of us. I soothed myself with my reasons as I took deep breaths to gain more control of myself. Once I settled in myself, I flushed and cleaned the toilet, rinsing my mouth and splashing water on my face.

"You okay, Lily?" Mary asked, pushing the door open. "I'm sorry. I didn't mean to put that on you. You had a lot to deal with back then. You were in your first relationship. You were in love. I mean, you planned to marry that asswipe," she said, clenching her fists.

I took a deep breath. "I can only say I'm sorry, Mare. Yes. I lied to you all and I'm sorry … I did what I thought was right … I'm not perfect."

"None of us are," Mary said. "I'm only upset because I didn't know, and I didn't help you. I've been a terrible friend."

I gripped her shoulders. "No, you haven't. I've been a terrible friend to you. Just know I'm sorry."

"Stop apologizing," Mary grumped. "I hope Declan goes to jail. I'm going to put a protest together to boycott his business."

She pursed her lips.

"All the way in New York? Stop, Mary. He was arrested, and I won't speak to him again. I think that's enough."

I walked past her, and together we walked down the hall to her bedroom. I flopped down on the four-poster bed that took up most of her room.

"He will get the message and leave me alone. I really just want to put it all behind me," I repeated.

I sat up and looked at her, wincing at the hostility on her face. While I was ready to move on, Mary wasn't.

"Why are you so certain he won't try anything else?"

she asked. "He hit you in broad daylight. He came to your job."

My stomach knotted. "Can we please talk about something else for a little while?" I pleaded.

"Okay," she finally conceded. "You're right. We should process."

I closed my eyes and she hugged me. She paused as she eased her hand on the back of my shirt and felt along my spine. I edged away.

"Seriously. You're perfect just the way you are," Mary said quietly.

I moved my hair to hide my face and laughed. Mary didn't join me, sitting down next to me instead. I reached in my pocket and checked my phone, looking for a distraction. I had two texts—one from Ian, and the other from Dani. No Jonas. My shoulders drooped, but I read the messages anyway.

Hi, Lily. My friend Diane will be calling you soon about pressing charges. How about dinner tomorrow night? As friends :)

Ian was persistent. I quickly texted back.

I'm in Boston with my friend Mary. I'll have to pass on dinner. Sorry.

Next was Dani's.

Hello, Lily I spoke with Jonas. I'm... sorry. Give him time. If you want to talk, I'm here.

The pain cut me down so far I wondered if I'd ever be able to rise up again. Knowing he had discussed my feelings with Dani, while keeping his own promise to stay away from me, hurt. But it was her "sorry" that gutted me. It made it feel so … final.

"Okay. Now the most important question of the afternoon. *First Contact* or *The Search for Spock* as we work on my papers?" Mary asked, knowing I needed something else to focus on.

I climbed off the bed. "*First Contact*, of course. Duh."

I lowered my head to protect my heart, as I wasn't ready to discuss the texts. But the second I settled across from Mary at the workstation she created in the dining room, she had me telling her what was on my mind once more.

"Let me play the Devil's advocate," she said once I had finished. "Jonas helped your funding for the legacy, flew you up to Connecticut, took you to meet his family, and went all territorial sex on you at an event. I'd say he's a bit more attached to you than he's letting on. So give him time. Give yourself time."

I focused on the computer screen without responding. Dani and Mary both wanted to give me hope where there wasn't any. Jonas was pretty clear in his intentions and had always been open and honest with me, unlike I had been with him.

"Does he even know what happened to you?" she asked in a soft tone, bringing my attention back to her.

"No. And before you protest, I will tell him. But in my own time. When I feel better and have some distance from it all myself. And from what Dani and Ian said, he'd freak out anyway. I don't want that."

I shuddered.

"I'd pay to watch him go medieval on that asswipe," Mary said, venom dripping from her voice.

I laughed. "You have quite the vocabulary there, Ms. Stoebe."

"Why, thank ya very much, Ms. Salomé," she said in her best Elvis impression.

She added a few lip curls and pelvis twitches that made me laugh even harder. This time she joined me.

Once we recovered, I said, "I don't love Declan anymore, but I don't want to hurt him, either. I just want him to get help and leave me alone. As far as not telling Jonas, I don't want him to be with me out of pity."

Mary nodded. From her expression, I could tell she didn't agree with me, but I also knew she would respect it. She did this by not saying another word, both of us diving into her sociology coursework instead.

CHAPTER ELEVEN

OVER THE LAST few days I had found myself on a crash course through Mary's sociology master's degree program. I had forgotten how much researching went into the mere selection of a quote for a paper. Her jam-packed schedule made the days full and occupied my mind. I needed the distraction since I still hadn't heard from Jonas after my love grenade.

"You're up already?" Mary asked.

This was quickly becoming our morning routine, though I had only been at her place for three days. I would get up at dawn to go run, and she would grouch about it. Her apartment was in a renovated Victorian house and her small section on the bottom front was cozy. Any movements on the creaky wooden floorboards blared like a foghorn—at least to Mary. Not to mention the fact that she was a light sleeper, something that had irritated me as her college roommate. Waking her up had always required an explanation, even if it was something as mundane as "my feet were cold so I opened my dresser to get socks. Go back to sleep." Her drowsily turning over after said offerings was the only reward.

I loved Mary, but I couldn't wait to return home this afternoon. I missed being in my own space. I missed New York.

Mary alternated between concerns and disappointed looks, while we worked on her papers. She'd ask on a loop, "Why did you stay with Declan?" Of course, none of my reasons were ever good enough. This scrutiny was exactly why I had hidden what he did to me from her and my parents. How many ways could I say I gave him chances because I loved him and believed he loved me? My reasons gave her only more room for debate, as she drilled home how wrong I had been and what I should have done. The only break I found from her inquiry into my psyche was running.

"I'll be back in half an hour or so," I announced.

I crept around the room, changing out of my Conan O'Doyle T-shirt into a pair of borrowed jogging sweat-pants and a winter fleece jacket. I made a quick, messy piled bun of my hair, and did a few stretches. I grabbed my phone and made it out the door before Mary had a second wind grumble.

The freezing chill of the air hit me in the face as I ran down Beacon Street. Boston was under an arctic nor'easter. A few feet of snow lined my path along the streets. My insides warmed as I ran up Kirkland and then on to Francis Avenue toward Harvard Yard. The red-brick and stone buildings, perfectly situated trees, and awing specialty shops along the square made everything in Cambridge picturesque. I missed Massachusetts, my home.

My mind raced along with my pace, as I thought about my parents and their deaths. When my mind caught up, I realized I had auto-piloted to the MTA subway at the Square. I needed to see something. I purchased a pass and took the Redline train to Quincy Center. I knew I wasn't going to Hancock Cemetery, where my parents were buried, or the elementary school where my mother had taught, though, I would need to speak with Ms. Parker about the Salomé Legacy program soon. No. Right now, I was heading home.

Or what had been my home, I thought somberly, as I exited the subway and headed above ground to Quincy. A mile run had me rounding Franklin in no time. Steadying my pace, I slowed down and stopped before the two-story yellow brick colonial house on Franklin Street. The stonework was still the same, as were the large windows with black plantation shutters. Even the rose bushes planted by my mother were there, though now made barren by winter. The house looked inviting, but empty. Just like me.

A memory drifted before me as I stood there, as if it was imprinted in the house. It was a memory I would have stopped if I could.

I'm standing on the last step of our polished mahogany staircase in our small foyer. I'm staring at my mother, her long, black wavy hair foaming around her face and brushing her shoulders. She's wearing my father's favorite sky blue

V-neck blouse, the one that enhances her curves. In her hands is a floral Hermes's scarf to cover up. I laugh, knowing my dad would likely hide that. Her wide blue eyes were filled, threatening to spill over.

"Don't cry, Mom. It's only dinner. I'll be here the rest of the weekend," I say, wiping the smudged mascara under our shared large, silvery eyes.

"But you're always working now. You don't come up here enough," she replies.

I glance over her shoulder and saw my father, looking impeccable in a dark grey wool suit. His short grey hair perfectly parted. His mustache groomed and trimmed, He's handsome and flawless.

He juts his chin at me as his dark eyes scan me from head to toe. "Ever the vagabond." He tugs my messy ponytail. "What are we going to do with you, Tiger Lily?"

I lower my gaze and pull my hair down. "I'm going to the salon on Monday."

"That's Monday. How about doing something about it today?" He tucks my hair behind my ears. "Your mother is right. We barely see you anymore."

I sigh. "I was here two weeks ago."

"But that was for the Stevenson's fundraiser," My mother says.

I bit my lip. "I can't come up every week."

"This isn't like you, Lily. Is this because of him? You can bring him up here. What was his excuse for not coming this time?" He smirks. My mother groans.

"His name is Declan, Dad. He has his business to run. I told you. He was too busy to come...."

My father snorts. "But he can drive from New York to pick you up from here?" He turns his head toward my mother. "Now he has her making up excuses for him."

"Leave her alone, Randall," She scolds.

He turns back to me and frowns. "You're lying for him. Salomé's don't lie. Especially not to each other. We raised you better than that."

I stare down at my feet. "That's what he told me. He has to be on hand just in case they need him at his store. I don't know. I'm sorry."

"Lily," He says and I look up at him. "I'm not trying to upset you. I miss you. We miss you."

My mother moves over to me and puts her arm around my waist. "We do. It's not the same without you here. I'm sorry." She wipes the corner of her eye.

My eyes water. "I miss you both and I miss being here. How about I come back next week? I'll leave work early on Friday, but I'll have to leave early on Sunday?"

My mother's eyes light up. "That's great!"

"That's better," My father corrects. He leans in to kiss my cheek. "We'll call you when we leave the restaurant."

"We love you," Mom says as my father pushes her toward the door.

"Love you, Mom and Dad," I call out with a few silly kisses blown their way.

Mom grabs at those kisses as Dad waves from our black four-door sedan.

"See you soon, Tiger Lily," they call out as they drive away.

My heart ached at the replay of that last night together. The house was imprinted, haunted with the life we shared and the person I had been back then. Both were gone, never to return.

I re-built. I broke again.

Would I ever be able to have my own love and family again? I started to head away when my phone rang, breaking apart my grief. Reaching inside my pocket, I looked down at the screen.

Unrecognized number. The criminal lawyer again? I groaned. Though I was conflicted, I had to admire her persistence. I wish I had that kind of strength to stand up and fight against those that couldn't help themselves. People like me.

I wasn't sure what I was going to do, but I figured now was as good a time as any to deal with this. I sighed and pressed the button.

"Yes?"

"Lily. It's Jonas."

My breath caught and my pulse sped up. "Oh … Hello," I said, cursing myself for the lift in my tone.

"You love me," Jonas said, addressing the issue head on, though it had taken him three days to call.

"Yes. I do." I cleared my throat. A flutter went through my chest. "I believe I do love you, Jonas."

"I wish I was at 'I love you,' or wherever you need me to be, but I'm not. We haven't spent enough time together. I'm just divorced…."

I swallowed against the pain clawing my throat. "You

told me as much in the car. I only told you because I wanted you to know how I feel about you."

"I just think we haven't spent enough time together," he said.

The sound of cars driving by filled my ears and I raised my voice to speak over it. "I know."

I didn't know what else to say to him.

"You on your way back?" he asked.

"No. I will be in a few hours, once I get to the station and get a ticket back." I sucked in air. "I'm ... I'm actually outside my old home in Quincy," I said, and my voice wavered.

"You shouldn't be there alone," Jonas said in a soothing tone. "If I knew you wanted to go there, I would have gone with you."

"It wasn't exactly planned. I was jogging and I just ... I wanted to see the house again. It just felt odd to be here and not do something to mark their memory ... Anyway, thank you," I said, pressing my feet in a snow bank.

"I'm about to leave for London. I decided to leave from New York instead of Texas. I sent someone else to oversee things in Texas in my place," he said, and from his tone I gathered this was a big deal for him to do. "I decided to go early, so I could get back to New York City myself as soon as possible."

"Oh. That's good news. I bet Dani and Paul will be happy to hear that," I said in a polite tone.

"There is something else," he said. "I ... I can't stop

thinking about you. I missed you the minute I left Mary's. I missed you. I wanted you to know I do care about you. I feel for you. I just don't know what those feelings are."

A warmth went through me at his words, but what did they mean?

"Say you'll see me when I return to New York as friends," he said. "Give us a chance to spend more time together outside of a companionship."

I licked my lips. "We'd see each other as friends?"

"Yes. I don't want to hurt you. I want to get to know you outside of an agreement. I set things in my life in a way I can handle them. If you're my companion, I'd expect sex and friendship. If you want to explore … feelings, I don't want to complicate it more than friend-ship. Dani and I were friends before we dated and married."

I felt like the ground had fallen out from under me. He was going to consider me like he did with Dani. I wasn't sure my heart could handle him letting me go again, but he seemed willing to try for me. A ray of hope sparked inside me.

"So, we would see each other as friends. Would we be seeing anyone else?" I asked.

I left off sexually, as I feared the answer.

Jonas didn't say anything, and the message hung in the air. He would get another companion, but be friends with me. Getting to know me, didn't mean exclusivity. It wouldn't be a relationship. It would be a new level of friendship. But was I willing to watch him with someone else and not me? Was I expecting too much? Everything spun around in my head.

"I'll be open and honest with you, and I'll expect the same back. If I were to take on a new companion ... we'll discuss it," Jonas offered.

"Yes. I miss you and want to try your friendship. But honestly I don't think I could handle seeing you with someone else, Jonas," I confessed.

"We'll talk about it when I return," he said in a gentle tone. "I want to see you in a way that we both could handle. So?"

"Okay," I said. "Yes. I'd like that."

"Good." He exhaled into the phone. "I'm glad."

"Me, too," I replied.

I felt like a weight had lifted off me.

"There is something else I want you to agree to," he said.

"What's that?" I asked, toeing the snow in the bank before me.

"I want to know what you're not telling me. So when I come back, my expectation is that you tell me. Whatever it is, Dani and Ian aren't saying ... This hurts Dani. She feels ill keeping things inside. I want to know what's going on and if I can help you."

I rubbed the center of my chest. I knew the feeling. I didn't want to hurt Dani. But after Mary's reaction, I also didn't want to tell him. I wanted to be seen as strong, like Dani, and able to handle and solve things without his pity or interference.

"I'm afraid to tell you," I finally said, my voice almost a whisper.

"That's a start. And it pleases me you admitted to that," he said. "We'll work on the rest."

I bit my lip. "Why me?"

"Why do I want to try with you?" Before I could respond, he said, "You're beautiful, smart, sweet, and gentle. You also have a little fire in you I can't resist. I can't stop thinking about the way you stood up for me against Vincent. You listen and have a giving heart—you took on the youth art program despite your limited resources. You're easy to talk with ... must I go on?"

"Oh please," I grinned.

He paused and his voice softened. "There is something there between us. I don't know what it is yet, but I want to try to find out."

I would have given anything to wrap my arms around him. But I doubted this friendship idea of his would work when we were together, and I told him so.

Jonas made a low sound that caused a tremor to run through my body. "I doubt it, too, but we can try. But there is one more thing I want to make clear. Ian is off limits."

I parted my lips. "We negotiating?" I teased.

"Not up for negotiation," he said, in his what I'd come to know as his "I mean business" tone.

"Not even coffee?" I couldn't help but tease him again.

"Lily. I'm serious," Jonas said, annoyance in his voice.

"You have nothing to worry about outside of friendship," I assured.

"I'm not worried about you, but I know Ian, and he's interested. I don't want you to see him outside of when you're with me," he said.

I grinned. He was going all possessive, and it thrilled me. I liked the idea of him wanting me all for himself as I felt the same way about him.

"Okay. I won't do anything with Ian without you." The sound of a car speeding past had me speaking louder into the phone as I paced a path on the sidewalk. "I wish I could see you now."

I squeezed my eyes shut. The words escaped my thoughts and I couldn't take them back.

"I wish I could come back right now," Jonas replied.

I let go of the breath I was holding.

"Even if I'm not physically there, I'm here for you. Call me anytime. Regardless of the hour. I'll make time for you," he promised.

I swallowed against the lump in my throat. "Thanks. You can call me, too."

"Good. See you soon, Tiger Lily," Jonas said.

I smiled as I took one last look at my home and headed back up Franklin Street.

"See you soon, Jonas."

CHAPTER TWELVE

B Y THE TIME I reached Mary's apartment, there was a text waiting for me from David.

You have an open ticket from Boston to Newark waiting for you at the airport. I'll pick you up in arrivals. Mr. Crane said it's bought and can't be refunded.

I shook my head, though I was smiling. Jonas was back and he was already taking over. The fact that he had reached out, and was willing to consider the possibility of us, clouded any of my annoyance at his overseeing my transport back to New York. Strangely, I found it comforting. Perhaps I was giddy over the possibility.

Jonas's offer of friendship was a step forward. He was seeing me as more than a sexual partner. He missed me and couldn't stop thinking about me. He had feelings for me. My mind skipped over the part I wasn't ready to handle—Jonas would choose a new companion to fulfill his sexual needs to avoid mudding the waters with me. Instead of dwelling on the negative, I floated in the possibility.

I skipped up the steps and put the key in the lock. As I swung open the door, my feet bumped into a bag and I almost tripped. On further examination, I realized it was my bag.

"Mary?" I called out.

Mary came into the living room like a whirlwind, her coat swinging around her body, my coat in her hand.

"You took an extra-long run today," she said as she handed me the coat. "I have class tonight. Did you forget? I can only drive you to the train station if we leave right now." She paused long enough to say, "Unless you want to stay an extra day? You're, of course, welcome."

I smirked. Mary had warned me about her schedule and I had promised to not take too long for the run last night, but I still teased her. "Doesn't look like it."

"I'm sorry." She bit her bottom lip. "We planned it last night and I'm sorry to do this to you. I didn't want to pack you, but I didn't want you lugging everything on the bus or wasting money on a taxi. If you want to stay, you can. I want you to stay."

She reached for my bag and started rolling it back toward her bedroom.

"Stop, Mary," I said and laughed. "I was only joking. I just hoped for a shower and to pack up, or for us to have a coffee together or something, but that's fine. I took longer than normal, so it's my fault."

I picked up my handbag and took the handle of my trolley from her to roll it back toward the door.

"I already feel guilty packing you and you're teasing me," Mary said, but relief crossed her face. "I'm still sorry, but thanks for understanding."

We shuffled out of the house. I handed her the key, then remembered it was my spare, and put it back on my key ring.

"You know, I don't have a key to your bachelorette pad," Mary said.

She opened her trunk and loaded her large, overfilled backpack and my trolley bag. I could have sworn I gave her my set of spare keys.

"Come visit me in New York sometime and I'll be sure to get you another one," I countered. "Because I'm assuming you must have lost the one I gave you last year?"

"I don't have your keys," Mary said simply, then added, "So we're off to South station?"

"Actually, I'm going to the airport."

She shot me a quizzical look. We both knew plane tickets were twice as much as taking the train.

"I was late getting back because I was talking to Jonas," I explained. "He sent me a ticket. And he ... wants to talk when he returns. As friends."

She beamed at me. "Good. He came to his senses, just took him a few days." She climbed inside the car and I followed suit, buckling myself in my seat. "Friendship, eh? Make him stick to it."

I looked out the window. "And just how am I supposed to make that happen?" It was more a rhetorical question, so I continued, "He said he wanted to talk. So that's a start, I guess."

"You're going to tell him about Declan, right?" Mary asked as she started the car.

"I'll handle it," I assured her.

She blew out a puff of air. "Talk it out. If you don't trust him, then you shouldn't be with him. You deserve the best, Lily."

I closed my eyes. She meant well and I appreciated it, but she was also back to lecturing. "I didn't even get a shower," I whined, signaling a change in the subject.

Luckily, Mary bit. "The other runs were a half hour. You were gone almost two hours this time." She shrugged as she drove down the road. "So, where did you go?"

"I went to Quincy," I said. "Back to the old house. I just ... I wanted to see it again."

"Oh. I'm sorry, Lily," Mary said.

Sadness enveloped the car as she drove on. It only got worse when we reached the highway, not far from where my parents had died.

I sought a distraction and texted David back, letting him know I was in compliance and on my way to the airport. Then I reached out and turned on the radio. I pressed Mary's CD player, and *Heart* filled the car. She sped past the spot of my parents' death and started singing. We took turns belting lyrics the rest of the drive to the airport.

Mary pulled up to the five-minute stopping point and we quickly unloaded. We looked at each other, and I laughed at the mismatched outfit she had on. She wore a flannel, long gypsy skirt, and a pair of cowboy boots along with a side ponytail circa the 1980s. I giggled, and told her exactly why.

"At least I showered," Mary said, jutting her chin.

"Love you, Mare bear," I said with a smile.

She gave me a lethal look. I knew she didn't like her family nickname, but we both enjoyed teasing each other.

"Love you, too, Tiger Lily," she finally replied. "Call me when you get back."

I took her hug and waved her off as she drove to Boston College. I already missed her as I went into the terminal and up to the ticket counter. I typed in the e-ticket confirmation number David had texted me.

My flight was due to leave two hours later, but boarded a good forty minutes early. I used the time to check my work email and send some responses to Gregor. I sat down in my seat on the plane and felt relieved. I missed New York City and my life there. I wanted my apartment, my shower, and my bed.

When we arrived in Newark, I rushed through security as quickly as I could and was jovial when I saw David there waiting for me. I was even poised when I climbed inside the car and sent a dutiful text to Jonas, letting him know I had arrived. I was practically beaming with the possibilities. Ten days and he'd be back here with me.

The sun was hot on my back as I climbed out of the car twenty minutes later at my apartment. I convinced

David to hand over my bag once I was inside my building. As soon as I got off the elevator, I dug through my bag for my keys, only to find the door already open. I was even more surprised when I found my roommate, Natasha, there on a work afternoon. She was standing in a T-shirt cooking breakfast. The aroma of bacon and eggs had my mouth watering, but nothing about this meal was on my diet plan. Or Natasha's.

"You're off work today," I said, stating the obvious. "I didn't know you cooked."

"I cook," she snipped. "The office didn't have heat so we were sent home early. Where have you been the last few days?" She raised her brow. "With Ian?"

A small smile appeared on my face. She remembered his name from the gala night.

"I was in Boston. I thought I sent you a text?"

"You didn't," she said and shrugged.

I frowned. I should have at least let her know. *Self-absorbed*, I thought, denigrating myself. "Sorry."

I rolled my cart down the hall and paused when I opened my door. My lamp was on and my duvet was flipped back again. I could have forgotten once, but twice? I dumped my stuff and headed back to the kitchen.

"My light was on in my room and the duvet was up on the side. I thought I put it back down before I left the other day. Did you borrow something?" I asked.

Natasha frowned. "Why would I go in your room? The only thing worth borrowing is your trolley bag and you took that with you." She paused, seeming to think for a moment. "I didn't notice the light on when I ran this morning. Maybe it's broken."

I chewed my lip. "Maybe ... Okay. If you see it on would you mind turning it...?"

A sickening thought hit me. I stopped mid-nag and headed back toward my room.

"What's going on?" Natasha called after me.

I didn't answer. Instead, I continued back toward my bedroom. My mind started to race and my pulse sped up. I didn't know if I was overreacting or underreacting, but I couldn't settle the paranoia rising in me.

I combed through my room, checking to see if anything else was out of place. It wasn't perfect, as I had rushed to pack, but this disorder wasn't all from me.

It didn't take long for me to find that the papers in my container were open and some of my photos were out of the album. I pulled it off the shelf and grabbed my chest. The bookshelf displayed an empty space where the copy of *Peter Pan* my father had given me should have been. Tears started pouring down my cheeks, as I threw every book on the floor. I upended the container with my papers and photo albums in search of the book, not willing to accept it was out of my possession.

I had shown it to Jonas recently, but had quickly returned it to the bookshelf. That was exactly where it should have been now.

As I flipped frantically through the photo album, I noticed the picture Declan had left with the flower delivery the day after he had attacked me. It was now ripped in half. Next to it was another photo—one of me in a bathing suit that was taken six weeks after my parents' death. My eyes hovered over the swelling in my face and the bloating of my body. I had smiled for the first time in that picture. But when I saw it, I begged him to delete it from his camera. He had refused, "joking" that I was being a "fat, spoiled princess."

And now, this picture was sitting in front of me – with those same words scrawled across it.

That was when I accepted the inevitable and screamed.

"What are you doing?" Natasha asked. She had followed me into my room, and shook her head at the disarray. "Look at this place. You've lost your mind."

I closed my eyes tightly. "Declan was here. Somehow. He hit me and now he broke in and stole—"

"Wait … he hit you?" Natasha interrupted. Then, as the realization overtook her, she continued, "You lied and told me you fell, but I'm no fool. I knew someone had hit you. I heard your friends talking about it when they came over a few weeks ago." She pursed her lips. "I thought, 'Fine. Okay, she doesn't want to admit it,' but I didn't think you were stupid enough to not check your keys or do anything to protect yourself from him after."

My eyes opened and I winced under the hostile look she gave me. My stomach churned. She was right. I hadn't thought it through.

"How did he get in here?" she asked.

I ran my hands down my arms repetitively as she paced, her disgust palpable.

"He must have had my spare key. I don't know, but I'll find out. I'm sorry," I stammered. "I did go to the police. It's fine. I'll call him. It'll all be fine."

"It's not fine," Natasha said. "*I* was alone in the apartment. What if I walked in on him? What if I came back while he was in here and he wanted to keep me quiet?"

My stomach clenched. I didn't have any answers to give her. "I'll get the building to change the locks. It's fine. You're not hurt. He only wanted to hurt me."

She twisted her mouth. "No. *You* put *me* in danger—"

"I didn't mean to," I cut her off. "Look, Declan wouldn't do anything to you. He was after me, not you. He's upset because I got a restraining order and he was arrested."

Her eyes widened. "Arrested? This is serious. How could you be so selfish and stupid?" she spat. "I can't live with someone this stupid."

"I'm not stupid. This isn't about you. If he was after you, he would have…." I spluttered.

She glared at me and I changed the course of my argument. "I will get the locks changed and that will settle everything."

Natasha gave me a look, as if I was a stranger. "I never thought you, of all people, would do this to me. But I'm not your bitch. I'm leaving."

"We have three more months here. You can do

whatever you want after that. You can't break the lease."

My eyes narrowed.

She lifted her chin. "I will and I can. I'm telling the building manager what you did and they will get me out of the lease. I'm not staying where I'm not safe."

She turned and walked out of my room. I followed after her to her bedroom, where she closed the door in my face.

I rapped on the door. "Come on, Natasha. Let's talk this through. Don't do this. You know I'd go through my savings trying to keep this place on my own."

Natasha spoke through the door. "There is nothing left to discuss. You won't be able to change my mind. I'm not risking my life or my stuff for your psychotic ex. Now, I'm calling the manager. You just better hope they let you stay here after I tell them what happened."

My heart pounded in my chest as my mind raced along with all the things that were unfolding before me. I had fucked up. It was my responsibility. I had known all along we weren't going to renew together, she wanted too badly to live in Manhattan. But now my own status in this place might be in question. When I heard Natasha connect her call, I turned and walked back into my bedroom and closed the door.

Shrinking in on myself, I sat down on the floor. *The lie that grew into more lies.* When would I ever learn? A lie that almost cost my friendship with Mary, had shamed my parents' memory, lost me my roommate and now may get me in financial trouble with my building.

Would they evict me?

All for Declan. Anger welled up inside me. I threw things around until I found my phone and called the demon that kept haunting me. Declan. He answered on the first ring.

"So, I'm no longer blocked now, you stupid fat bitch?" he seethed.

"I don't want to talk to you, but you need to know. You broke in here. My roommate called the manager. So you may make your situation worse," I hissed. "Now, give me the keys and return my book,"

"I was arrested. Me? At my business!" Declan said, ignoring me. "You better *hope* I'm not arrested again. You *better* tell them you forgot you told me to pick something up for you or I'll rip this book to shreds."

My body shook as I gripped the phone. He knew that book held a lot of meaning for me. It had been my father's gift of pure love, and inspiration, and held some of my most precious memories. It had even connected Jonas and me on our first night together when he had awakened within me that feeling of being cherished and cared for. Yes, Declan indeed had in his possession something I would risk everything to have returned to me.

"Did you like the photo?" Declan asked and laughed derisively. "I've got more, too … some you haven't seen. Some with a little less than that suit."

"No you don't. You're lying," I said with doubt in my voice.

"Risk it and see. I'll send them to your boss or post them online. Try me," Declan said.

My face crumbled. "No. Please don't. I'm sorry. I'll make this right," I repeated over and over, a broken record.

Truly, I had come apart. After a while, I finally quieted.

"You done?" he chuckled.

"Why do you hate me?" I asked, my voice so small.

"Hate you? No. I don't hate you. I love you. I still love you and still want to marry you. I did this to help you understand how much it hurt to find out you tried to destroy my life. But now, I forgive you," Declan said.

"Please, don't do this," I sobbed.

"Shhh. It's over now," he cooed. "I wish I was there to hold you."

I wiped my cheek. "I don't know what I can do. It's out of my hands now. I made a mistake. I didn't think … I didn't want to ruin your life."

"You never think. You let everyone else think for you. I found it exhausting having to think for you all the time," he said.

I sniffed. "Will you return my book?"

"I'll hold it until you do the right thing," Declan said. "My having it with me will remind you that if you betray me again, I'll betray you, too."

In my heart, I knew this was all a game to him. And that I may never see that book again.

Be like Dani, I thought. Be strong.

I so wish I could be.

My mind gave way to fear, conjuring up memories of him abusing me. His hands and his words. Memories I didn't want to relive again. How could I stop this from happening? I would have to do what he wanted. I would give in again. *I already made the decision*, my mind crowed. Why was I fighting? I tried to soothe myself as I prepared for the inevitable. I was going to give in. Still, I couldn't stop the words that fell from my lips in my own quest to hurt him.

"You may not hate me." My voice wavered. "But I … hate you. You won't give me that book back anyway. Just stay the hell away—"

"Stop the dramatics." His voice was like ice. "I want those charges off my record. Now. I've got no more time to waste. I work."

He hung up, and I sat frozen on the floor, unable to move.

The slam of the front door broke my trance, and I winced as the pain on my hand registered. The line was as empty as I felt. I had made a mess of everything. Natasha had left. What other choice did I have left? Declan wasn't going to stop. What if he did something to Natasha? Or someone else to hurt me? I needed to make to make everything right. *I need to get him out of my life.* The only way that had worked in the past. The only way I knew how.

I had to give him what he wanted.

I dialed the building and got Carla, the building

manager, on the phone to use the lie given to me.

"I understand, Lily. However, if he broke in, as your roommate Natasha said, it is a police matter."

"He didn't. I take full responsibility. It wasn't Declan's fault. I ... I gave him the keys. Nothing was ... stolen. It was a mistake. I am going down to the station to drop the restraining order. I really overreacted. I'm sorry."

"Well, you will need to fill out an incident report," she said. "You will also have to cover the fees for lock changes. You're roommate has requested to move out and we plan to grant that move to her. You will need to cover her security deposit, after she schedules her walk through and we check the apartment. Any new tenants would have to be approved and meet our requirements. If you move anyone in without our permission, you will not be allowed to renew your lease. Do you understand?"

"Yes. I'm sorry," I said hoarsely.

Who would move in for three months? Then again, I wasn't going to be able to afford to stay past that on my own.

"We're sorry, too, but we have to consider the safety of our building," she said and ended the phone call.

I slowly started cleaning my room. I went about the apartment, cleaning it for hours. By the time I was done cleaning, everything was sparkling. I went back to my bedroom and curled into a ball, finally falling asleep. When I woke, I heard my phone beeping with a text from Natasha.

Ari offered me a place in Manhattan. Movers will come for my stuff.

I won't be back.

Everything was ruined. *Again*, I thought morosely, as I went to my bedroom and changed into my sweats. I exercised hard, until my whole body hurt as much as I hurt on the inside. I then went across the hall and showered, scrubbing myself raw, but not clean. I was dirty. My lies made me dirty, filthy. My phone beeped and I took it out to check the messages.

I found missed calls from Dani, Ian, the criminal lawyer, and Jonas. I licked my lips and erased all the messages that had been left without listening. Once they found out I planned to drop the charges, they would all be gone anyway. No amount of their inquiries or pressures would change my mind now, though.

Declan had won. Again. I was going to do what he wanted from me.

My heart constricted at the weight of all that my actions had cost me. I continued to underestimate him. I continued to lie and deceive. The more I thought about the people I loved, the book, photos, and memories, the more the pain inside me grew, spreading out and bringing me to my knees. I found it so overwhelming that all I could think about was needing it to go somewhere. I needed some way to channel it away before it crippled me. I had never been prepared or groomed for this in my small world in Quincy with my parents. They'd sheltered and protected me. They had wanted me to be perfect and I tried. I tried my best.

I started running in place, pushing myself harder and faster. I moved on to lunges, then crunches. Over and over again until sweat covered my body and the pain in my limbs screamed. I'd fix this and my life. *I'll fix everything.*

I forced myself further still until I finally collapsed in exhaustion. But I wasn't thinking anymore, was I? I was numb. I was free.

CHAPTER THIRTEEN

I CLOSED THE door and bolted the new locks in place, marking the end of my first week alone in my now own personal, suddenly way out of my price range, loft apartment in Jersey City. At least, it was mine for the next few months.

Natasha had indeed moved out of our apartment and into Manhattan. To where, I wasn't sure. She hadn't answered any text messages from me. Not since our fight in my bedroom, where the truth of my situation with Declan had come out and cost me. She didn't feel safe here. In truth, neither did I.

I had lied and covered up everything again, to protect myself and the things dear to me. Not just things, but also the people I love and care about. Declan used to be on that list, but now he sought at every turn to hurt me.

My stomach cramped and I attempted to soothe it with my hand. Was it stress or was I hungry? *When did I last eat?*

My mind flashed on the unflattering picture Declan had left of me—the one labeled, "fat spoiled princess." I walked over to the refrigerator and took out a bottle of water, draining it. I was full.

My cellphone alerted me to a new text message, breaking through my negative thoughts as I reached inside my handbag. A trickle of fear went through me at the thought it might be Declan again, but instead I found a voicemail from Mary.

"Are you avoiding me? I've called and left messages. Did something else happen? I'm sorry I wasn't as available during your visit to Boston as I wanted to be, but I'm done with finals and can come up next weekend to do whatever you want. I miss you. Please call me."

I rubbed the center of my chest and sent a text reply.

I'm busy with work and everything. Sorry I haven't phoned back. I can't do next weekend. I'll be in touch soon.

Kicking off my shoes, I stared at the kitchen island. I had forgotten to put away the two dry cleaning bags that were there. One contained the dress I stained from the gala, which I had paid for the cleaning on. The other one had a black Chanel suit I had seen Natasha wear to work on occasion. I spread my hand over her note, pinned to the front of one of the bags, and read the message for the fourth time this week.

I can't fit these. You can have them. Natasha

I knew she could fit them, but it was as much of a peace offering as I would get. I couldn't fault her. She had been right. I didn't know what Declan would have done if he had found her here. And in good conscience, I couldn't bring someone else here while he was still focused on punishing me. Not even Mary.

I exhaled long and sent a text to Natasha. Our goodbye.

I'm sorry for what happened. I hope you enjoy your new place and I wish you the best.

I didn't wait for a reply. Instead, I just deleted her from my contact list. After all, we weren't friends. We were acquaintances, at best. I wasn't going to hear from her again.

My mood soured as I walked to my bedroom. The one place I used to look forward to returning to everyday had become the place I avoided. Nothing remained in here that I cared about, having carefully stored away all photos and videos that were left in my possession. The room was stripped down to the minimum. The taint of his theft was ever present, and I couldn't stand to be in the room for longer than a few minutes.

Prickly heat broke out on my skin as I removed my clothing in the dark and dumped the various articles in the laundry. I picked up my T-shirt and sweatpants, along with the folded blanket and pillows I had left there in the morning, and quickly exited the room. Returning to the living room, I put together my bed—simply a sheet, blanket and pillow on the couch for sleeping. My new routine.

It was a routine I had created to get through my days. At dawn every day, I ran the same route Natasha used to take me on, along the boardwalk in Jersey City. During lunch, I ran for an hour at the corporate gym. And now, I planned to change into my T-shirt and sweats and workout until I exhausted my thoughts enough to fall asleep. My mind kept replaying the question of why I had gone to the police department and dropped the charges. Why I told the building I gave Declan the key. Why I wasn't taking Dani, Ian, or Mary's phone calls. Or the numerous ones left by the man I loved, Jonas Crane.

My heart constricted and my eyes watered over my avoidance. I turned on the TV to drown out my thoughts. Part of me didn't want to hear their disappointment, though it was still evident in their voice messages. But in my heart I believed they had helped me enough, and I had to be strong and keep them safe until I found a way to rid Declan from my life completely.

As I slipped my T-shirt over my head, my phone chimed. I finished putting on my shirt, and walked over to the phone and frowned. Ian. Again. I was being cruel, my mind crowed. So, I decided to answer, if only so that I could give him the closure to let me go.

"Hello?"

"There you are." Ian's tone held a bit of sarcasm. "I thought I'd have to talk to the voicemail again."

"I've been busy," I said, as I balanced the phone on my shoulder and pulled on my sweatpants.

"Yes. I know. Diane said you dropped your restraining order."

"I did," I said, putting the sweatpants in place with one hand. "I didn't want him arrested, and, well, I'm fine now. I doubt I'll see him again. I'm considering moving back to Massachusetts." I *was* considering it, as a backup if nothing turned around here. At least, that was what I told my conscience. "There are other publishing houses up there and I'd be close to my charity," I offered in explanation.

"You don't have to *lie* to get rid of me," Ian said bluntly.

Bile rose in my throat, as his words stung me to the core. Lying was what I was known for now.

"I understand why you're avoiding me," Ian continued. "I am upset by your choice, but I had hoped we would be friends."

I found a pair of socks and sat down on the couch to put them on. "Yes. Well, I've got a lot on my mind with work and everything."

"I see," Ian said, disappointment coating his words. "Well, if you ever change your mind and want to watch a movie or have dinner or something, give me a call."

"I will. Thanks," I said.

I won't, I thought as I put on my sneakers.

He didn't acknowledge my promise, as he already knew me to be the liar that I was. "If anything happens again, don't hesitate to call me. You don't have to date me or be my friend for me to help you."

Too late.

"Thanks. I better go now," I choked.

"What's wrong, Lily?" Ian asked.

I took in a few short breaths. "Nothing. I'm about to workout."

I cursed myself internally. I had almost made it off the phone, but my weakness rose up and had to show itself so he could get involved and maybe pity me.

"You've been doing that a lot lately, huh? Every day at lunch, too?" he asked.

"How do you know that?" I chewed my bottom lip.

"David mentioned it to Dani," he said.

"Really?" I asked. "I told him he didn't need to drive me anymore."

"I guess Dani wants to have him keep an eye out anyway," Ian said.

"Does she now?" I asked and coughed. "Excuse me. Well, please tell her I'm fine."

"Avoiding her, too?" he asked with irritation. "You don't have to answer that. I apologize. I'm just worried about you."

I closed my eyes. "I'm fine. I'm about—"

"To workout," he finished my sentence for me. "Alright. Take care, Lily. And please remember what I said."

Ian hung up.

That went alright, I thought as I attempted to block out a wave of self-loathing. I was on my way to ending these thoughts racing through my mind. My routine.

I jogged, crunched, and squatted over and over again. Until everything stopped, and I was exhausted and ready for sleep.

Afterward, I sluggishly went to the shower and turned it on for a quick rinse. As I lathered, I noticed the hair growth on my body coming back in and my chipped nail polish. I grimaced. No waxing this month. It didn't matter. No one would be seeing me naked any time soon.

I climbed out and dried off, then went to the living room and unfolded the blanket and pillow on the couch. I walked over and checked the locks on the doors, then collected my phone again. Once the lights were out, I settled down on the couch for sleep, readying myself for that one piece of my routine that showed the chink in my armor of solitude. The one thing I couldn't bring myself to erase from my life just yet. In fact, it too had become part of my routine.

I held the phone to my ear and re-played my saved message from Jonas.

"Lily. This is my tenth call. I … This will be the last one. Friendships, companionships, anything—it all needs two to work. I accept you've changed your mind. As always, I'm here if ever you need a friend, Tiger Lily."

Jonas may be a minefield of rules and agreements, but I loved him. Still, love wasn't enough. Declan had taught me that, surely.

I didn't change my mind, Jonas. It was changed for me.

I wasn't ready to erase Jonas. My heart still craved him, wanted more than anything to be swept away into a life with him, but that was no longer a possibility. So I curled up in a ball, and pressed replay again. I focused not on the words, but his voice as it carried us where we could be together in my dreams.

The doorbell rings. Not a second later, the door flies open and my heart stops. It's Jonas, dressed in a navy business suit. My pulse increases with every step he takes as he strolls over to the couch.

"Strip and come to me," he commands.

My mouth forms a perfect "O."

"We'll get to that later," he muses.

"What are you doing here?" I ask.

His gaze burns over my body, heating me up as I quickly do as I am told, removing my clothes and walking over to stand before him.

"Good girl," he purrs in response.

"Don't call me that," I hiss.

He moves to stand behind me and pulls my arms up to his neck. He cups my breasts, kneading them as he breathes heavily against my neck. I moan and arch back against him, feeling his hard cock push against my ass through the thin fabric of his slacks.

"You are my good girl," he soothes. "You're always a good girl."

He pinches my erect nipples. I bite my lip and moan as he moves a hand down, stopping on my mound and trailing a finger through my slit. I part my thighs, willing him to take more.

"Always ready for me ... sweetie pie."

"Sweetie pie?!" I repeat in horror.

He laughs. My scowl turns into a moan as he teases me. Parting the lips of my sex with his hand and circling his finger around my clit. He pushes me over the back of the couch, runs his hand down my spine and over my ass.

"Don't move."

He unzips his pants and pulls out his cock, then rubs it against my pussy.

"Oh, Jonas," I moan.

As I push back, the tip of his cock enters me. He stops.

I look over my shoulder. "Jonas?"

"That's all you have time for." He grins.

My alarm went off, waking me from my dream. I let out a laugh at the silliness of the dream, though my heart felt heavy as I thought about Jonas and how much I missed him. I longed to be with him again. I even went as far as trying to convince myself that I should call him, but I stopped short of reaching for the phone. I couldn't be with him, and I couldn't let him go.

The next couple of weeks blended into each other. I was fully into my routine, and life went on, as everything always did in New York. Nothing stopped this city, and nothing stopped me. Or so I told myself.

I still checked my phone ten times a day for messages from Jonas, but found none. Jonas was true to his words and rules. But did he still think about me? My heart shriveled at the thought, but it was useless. Not with Declan still lingering. Nonetheless, Dani remained my link, never failing to send a text checking up on me. I eyed her most recent one as I sat on the PATH subway on my way home from work one Friday evening.

I'm very disappointed you didn't stick to our agreement, but I'll keep sending messages, Lily. Even if you don't respond. I'm here. We're here.

I took a deep breath and sent a message back.

Thank you.

A smile formed on my face as I leaned my head

against the window seat in the cold, crowded subway train. I couldn't help but admire Dani and her perseverance. I could see why Jonas stayed friends with her, even after their divorce.

My thoughts went back to the "we" part of her text. Did Jonas feel the same way? After all this time, I was sure he had moved on, as he'd told me he would. Still, I let the thoughts warm me as I stared out at the dark passage leading back to Jersey City.

CHAPTER FOURTEEN

I SAT AT my desk in the office and checked the time. I knew Declan was due back from lunch. I took a deep breath, and dialed his number. The call connected, but then went straight to voicemail like it had done since he'd broke into my place a month ago. The more I pursued him, the more he ignored me.

Declan. I've done all I can. You didn't stay in jail and the charges were dropped. Please, call me back and return my things.

These calls had become a regular part of my routine, as well as what came after. I choked and pressed "end" on the phone, then rose and ran to the bathroom, where I crouched down over the basin. My empty stomach cramped as I dry heaved. *Empty.* As empty as I felt, and my life was, now that I had pushed everything out of it all to get back to where I had been before I'd gone to Sir Harry's Bar to meet Jonas Crane.

My life had been easy then. It had been filled with old movies, games, and memories. There had been calls and visits between Mary and myself, working, and occasional movie nights with Gregor, and getting my hair done at Dee's. No Declan. No one, really. Unlike Gregor and Mary who had partners, I'd been alone and lonely. With only my memories to keep me company. But now even those were tainted by Declan. Oh, how I wish I'd never met him. I was trapped in his cruel game, and desperate to be rid of him for good. Hatred filled me, sickening my soul. I had work to distract me right now, but those thoughts all waited for me every evening.

I walked out the stall and went to the sink, where I rinsed my mouth and wiped under my eyes, smearing the cover-up makeup, then cursing myself for not remembering to bring it with me. The dark circles surrounding my eyes stood out from my pale skin, the result of my lack of sleep when exercising didn't work to exhaust me quite enough.

I fingered through my hair and noticed how brittle it was. I pulled some strands that fell on the top of the counter. My hair was falling out. It reminded me that I was going to see Dee at the salon. My life routine was returning. I exhaled and washed my hands before returning to my desk. Opening my handbag, I coated my cracked lips with gloss.

"Lily," Gregor said. I turned around and he gave me a smile that didn't quite reach his eyes. "Would you mind coming into my office?"

I raised an eyebrow at him, questioningly, but I rose and followed him inside.

"Close the door," he requested.

My heart pumped a little faster, as I squatted down

and removed the books holding the door open and closed it. I took the seat across from him. His solemn expression had me worried.

"Is there something wrong?" I asked.

"Yes," Gregor said and exhaled. "You, Lily."

My lips parted. "I've been ahead of schedule on all my projects. I worked all last week and over the weekend to make up for the time I missed in Boston. I have stayed late...."

"I'm aware of all that," Gregor cleared his throat. "It's not your job performance. I know Natasha moving out made things difficult. I am putting in a bonus this month that you very well earned. Your raise will have to wait for next quarter, though. Have you started looking for a new roommate?"

I lifted a shoulder. "I looked into it, but I don't know if I want to go through it again. My lease will end in a couple of months. I'm looking for a studio or efficiency in Queens and Brooklyn. I haven't found a place yet ... but it won't interfere with my work."

Gregor curved his lips upward. "I know and appreciate that." He exhaled. "Is there any other way I can help?"

I chewed my bottom lip. "I do need to ask for overtime. Anything you can give me, or if you know someone that needs help on the weekends...."

He tapped his pen on his desk as we sat quietly while he considered my request. After a few minutes he said. "Well, I could use some help here ... clearing up my office? I really could use the extra help organizing things here."

I grinned at Gregor and warmed at his sacrificing his "lucky" cluttered workspace to create a job for me. "Thank you, but I was thinking maybe some filing or typing. I could come on the weekends."

"What about your case?" Gregor paused and stared at me.

When it occurred what he was referencing. I eyed the papers in front of him.

"What case? There is no case anymore. All charges have been dropped, as far as I know. I haven't spoken to anyone."

"I know. Danielle Crane called me," Gregor said.

I licked my lips. "Please tell her she needn't worry. I just want to move on with my life."

"So no more Jonas?" he asked in a hushed tone.

A pang went through my chest. "We're friends."

"Oh, is that why you ... look different?" Gregor asked.

I raised my brows. "Whatever do you mean, Mr. Worton?" I joked.

He made a gesture around my face. "Your face looks pale, a little gaunt. You're wearing more makeup, your clothes ... you're not as put together as normal."

I looked down and blushed. My suit was a little creased, but otherwise I thought I looked okay. Ever the vagabond, Tiger Lily. I giggled and let out a sob at the same time.

Gregor's brows knitted together. "Lily, what's wrong?"

I covered my mouth. "Sorry. A joke I heard once." I shrugged. "I lost a little weight, but a new wardrobe is not something I can splurge on at the moment."

"I can give you a loan," Gregor said. "It'll come off your salary after you get settled again."

I lowered my head. "No. Thanks, Gregor. I'll get my clothing altered soon."

"Lily, I didn't mean to insult you, I'm just concerned. You look ill, tired. I'm just worried you've been working too hard. I'd give you stress leave if you needed it."

I sighed. Overtime and leave didn't go together. "I'm fine. A little tired, but really, don't worry about me."

"If you say so, Lily," Gregor said in a tone that said he didn't believe me. "I'll let you know today or tomorrow if any of the managers come back with extra work you can take home with you on the weekends."

I smiled at his added stipulations. "Thanks." I looked down at my watch as his gaze pressed on me. "It's close to my lunch appointment, and I can't be late. Dee gave me a special coupon for his favorite customers, when I tried to cancel with him."

Gregor smiled at me as he waved me out. I hurried and grabbed my handbag and coat, and left the office.

I was halfway to Herald Square at a fast pace, weaving almost effortlessly through the afternoon crowded pavement. The impromptu vendors sharing knockoffs, and tourists staring up at the buildings, were the only ones that slowed my steps as I slipped around them. I followed the flow of the rest of the New Yorkers on a path to our destinations. Mine was Dee Angelo's Salon.

I was looking forward to seeing Dee and getting a fresh new look. I breezed through the front door. I accepted a nod from Rachael, the receptionist, as I made my way around the reception desk to Dee's station. Dee was on his cellphone as I approached his black leather chair. His purple contact-colored eyes went wide, and his mouth dropped open. He motioned for me to remove my coat, and I hung it up on his coat rack.

"Who are you?" Dee asked as he greeted me.

His eyes squinted as he folded his arms.

"I'm ready for Mia Farrow."

The shocked look Dee gave me had me double over with laughter.

"You may be as thin as Mia was in that movie now," Dee said, his eyes scrutinizing me. "I think that suit is Chanel, but it looks like a bargain bin special hanging off you like that."

I pursed my lips, as I didn't have a good comeback. Dee was, as always, dressed in designer casual wear, a printed T-shirt and jeans.

"Hardly that thin, and you're right about the suit," I said, sticking out my bottom lip. "It's a parting gift from my ex-roommate, Natasha. I wore it to impress you."

"You look like the girl from that movie ... Tim Burton's *Corpse Bride*." He wrinkled his nose. "You're pale, your eyes look dead, and don't get me started on your skin. What's up with you? Because, girl, you need to rethink, rewind, and fix this shit."

I crossed my arms. "Hey, what happened to your policy of saying something positive to every customer?"

"I do when they need to hear it. But, lady, you need an intervention," Dee said, pausing for effect. I didn't know what to say as he patted my shoulder. "Even though I said I would love to cut this mane off, and I just may have to soon, since your hair is all uneven and broken off. There is no way I'm doing it when you're all messed up. Tell me what's going on," he said as he began wetting and trimming my hair.

I kept my tone relatively even as I filled him in on all the drama in my life, alluding to the physical assault and threats by Declan while placing more emphasis on my moving on, and putting everything behind me.

"Shit, girl. Where did you meet that loser?" Dee asked. "I've got a can of pepper spray you'll be leaving with today. We need to get some sleep in you. Get rid of those dark circles, and some meat on you to throw his ass down next time."

I shook my head and let out a sad laugh. "I've got plenty of meat, thanks."

He frowned at me as he finished up the cut and started styling my hair. "Girl, you're letting that piece of shit get to you. If we're talking about that ugly dude you were with a while ago, then he had no right to say shit. I mean, he was no model his damned self."

I lifted my chin. "So, according to your logic, only model hot men can treat us like shit?"

Dee smoothed down his hair. "No, not at all. I'm just saying, you're hot. And from what I saw of him when you were with him, he didn't have any right to throw stones, especially not at a beauty like you. Well, until you started messing with what you had working for you."

I snorted. "I came here for a lift, Dee. I'm going to give you a poor rating online for this."

He snickered. "You wouldn't dare."

We laughed together as he continued working on my hair.

After he was done, Dee bent down and hugged me. "I'm worried about you, girl. Take a long, hard look at yourself. You need to get it together. I better hear from you soon. Now, get back to work before your boss comes after you."

I couldn't answer around the lump forming in my throat, so I simply gave him a hug.

Once back outside, I drooped, and realized I was tired from my run and exercise the night before. I walked down the street, and picked up another lettuce and cucumber salad from the Korean deli and made my way to the office. As I walked inside, Olivia, stopped me at the front desk.

"Lily?" she asked. "You have a visitor waiting for you."

"Finally," a voice behind me exhaled.

I turned around and found Dani walking toward me from our small lounge. Her attire matched her demeanor; all business, from her designer black pants suit, to her blonde-bobbed hair in a slicked to her scalp ponytail. Her eyes squinted as they scrutinized me from head to toe. She stopped in front of me and her mouth turned down.

"I'm glad I caught you. I haven't seemed able to reach you by phone. Would you mind going for a coffee with me around the corner? I would love to catch up with you."

My mouth went dry as I stood in awe and envy of her strength. I fell under the power of her intention as I watched her put on her coat, readying herself as if I had already accepted her invitation.

I still tried to protest. "I just got back from a long—"

"I spoke with Gregor, and he assured me you could take the time," she said with a slight curve of her lips.

I sighed in defeat. I had been thoroughly ambushed by her.

"Okay."

I followed her out the door and down the street to the local chain coffee shop, where I ordered a plain coffee and she purchased a caramel latte. After we collected our drinks, we sat down in a two seat-table near the back.

"I had a speech prepared, but now that I see you, I can't bring myself to say any of it," Dani said. She took a sip from her cup. "I will say that I'm upset you went back on your agreement with me."

I glanced at her through my lashes. "I had … I dropped the charges. Declan hasn't come back to my office. The locks have been changed at my apartment. I haven't needed to do any deliveries at work, so I didn't think it was right wasting David's time…."

"Making sure you're safe is not a waste of time," Dani interjected. "It's important to me. You're important to me and Jonas."

Jonas. The mere mention of his name had my pulse racing.

"I don't understand how or why. You barely know me. And Jonas and I are not together anymore."

"I don't need a timeframe to care about you," she said softly.

I looked down at my cup in shame. "Even though I dropped the charges?" I asked, just above a whisper.

"Even though you dropped the charges." She covered my hands with hers. "I'm more upset that you disappeared, and I wasn't sure how you were doing."

She moved her hands back to her cup. I watched her take a sip, not knowing what to say next.

I finally said, "You may not need a time frame, but Jonas does … did. We're not together anymore … We're friends."

Dani's actions hadn't been that of someone who didn't care. She had gone above and beyond for me. I had avoided her to keep her away from all that was going on between Declan and me.

"I would hardly call it friendship when you refuse to

take his calls for weeks, and asking you to spend time with him doesn't mean he's asking for a timeframe," Dani said in his defense. She blew out. "Jonas has been miserable, to put it lightly. The time he had you around was pulling him out of all that. He was positively shining when you were together."

I swallowed hard. "I was happy with him, too, but that's not possible now."

"Well, I won't lie," she paused.

My face fell. *Like me.*

Her eyes clouded. "Jonas has pride, and yes, he has tried to move forward with Melissa...."

My heart shattered inside me and I found it hard to focus on what Dani was saying. Jonas had moved on from me, just as I had expected him to do. Just as I had pushed him to do.

"She can try to manipulate him," Dani was saying. "But it won't work, especially after that trip to Connecticut. I was sorry I wasn't able to go, but I understand you did. His mother was always cold to him. And, well, his father was demanding and controlling. He'd tried to shape Jonas into a miniature version of himself. Jonas thinks he's become him, but he hasn't. Maybe even because of you, he hasn't. Melissa can't give him what he needs."

I lifted my face to meet her eyes, which were staring intently at me. "What is that?"

"Love and compassion. Someone to care for," Dani said. "He has my love. And Paul's. But ... do you love him?"

Yes. That was the answer she seemed to want to hear above all else today.

"I do. He knows how I feel. I told him I loved him. I thought I did, anyway. But he was right. We haven't been together long enough for that."

We both sipped our drinks.

Dani finally said, "Why are you avoiding him?"

I stared at my cup. "I'd rather not say."

"Fair enough. You'll say it to him," Dani said. "Once he sees you, he will damned well insist."

My heart skipped a beat. "He's still in town?"

"Yes. He didn't go back to Texas," Dani said with a hint of amusement at my shocked expression. "I'll call him now, and let him know you're at the office."

I reached out and touched her arm, then pulled back. "Don't interfere." Then very quietly, I added, "Please."

Dani moved her chair next to me and put her arm around me. "Why are you afraid? You're about to get everything you want."

I gave her a confused look. "What do you mean by that?"

She only smiled. "I'll leave that for you to find out. You have also run out of time on telling Jonas about Declan. I'm telling him everything."

I shook my head frantically. "No, please. You can't."

She pressed her lips to my forehead. "You're warm. Are you feeling okay?"

I swiped the beads of sweat from around my hairline. "I'm a little tired."

Dani's eyes bore into mine. "From all that running."

I nodded, unable to speak. I knew she wasn't just talking about my physical exercise, or the fact that I was ill. I had been running for a long time. Running away, avoiding … lying. I was physically and mentally exhausted.

She gave me an empathetic look. "I don't like secrets. We have always been open and honest with each other. I can't do this to you or to him. So accept this and understand. I hope in time you will come to know I'm not doing this to hurt you, but to help you."

I opened my mouth and closed it. I could tell she had reached the end of her patience and was going to do this no matter what I said to her. And, though it angered me, I surrendered. Her posture was all-authoritative, but it softened as she studied me.

"Don't worry. Everything will work out."

She gave me a side hug then stood up, leaving me staring after her as she walked out of the café, her phone already at her ear.

I slowly walked back to the office. I busied myself at my station, but all the time my mind raced as I pondered what Dani was telling Jonas. What would he do? Would he care?

As the afternoon went on, I became weary, but then my phone chirped. My hand trembled as I read the message from Jonas.

He texted

No more avoiding me. It ends today.

CHAPTER FIFTEEN

I FELT MY pulse in my ears as I sat pinned to my office chair. Dani had told Jonas what happened and he was coming to get me. What his "getting me" meant, I didn't know. My cowardice had me wanting to flee before he came, but my exhaustion, along with my curiosity, had me remaining still. The truth was, I missed him. My love for him made me wait.

My phone beeped and my heart leapt. I fumbled as I took it to view the message. My heart stopped. It was a photo. This one was of me naked from the back, sleeping on Declan's bed. As I gazed in horror, a text message came in.

I showed this one to the guys at work today. Some of them would still do you. This is for all your text messages bothering me about your stupid stuff. You bother me. I'll bother you.

My body absorbed the weight of my thoughts as I placed my head in my hands. Dani was wrong. Jonas and I wouldn't get our time. Declan held my memories hostage and photos that could not only destroy me, but Jonas, too. Sure, he'd be prosecuted, but after the damage was already done, damage to my reputation, and

Jonas's. God, I cursed the day I ever met him.

The air shifted in the room and I didn't have to look up to know who was there. I felt him all over me. I lifted my head up and faltered.

"Jonas."

He stood there, a vision in a dark designer suit that tailored his frame impeccably. His crisp white shirt stood out from his tanned skin. His black hair was a little longer than I remembered a month ago, and fell back in waves, showing off an uninterrupted view of his prominent cheekbones and sensual, full mouth. As I met his eyes, our connection sparked, sending a shiver through me. His eyes turned stormy as he scanned me from head to toe. A frown deepened on his face with every step. I casted my eyes down. My heart beating hard against my ribcage as I waited for him to close the distance between us. My eyes followed his polished leather shoes out of the corner as he stopped behind me, trailing his hands down the side of my face and to my neck before settling them on my shoulders.

"What have you done to yourself, my Tiger Lily?"

I shuddered and closed my eyes. *His.* I could have wept. All I wished I could be.

"I don't know what I want to do to you more," he continued, his voice strained. "Scold or hold you. I'll decide later."

"Jonas Crane."

We both turned, and Gregor was standing in his doorway.

"Gregor," Jonas said.

He started to move his hands away, but paused as my body lifted up, not ready to part from his touch. He walked in front of me, and I trembled as his hand grazed my chin. I could avoid and deny all I wanted, but in front of Jonas, I was lost to him.

"I'm here to pick up Lily," Jonas said authoritatively, his body stiffening.

Their polite discomfort added to the whispers buzzing around the floor.

My face warmed as I looked at Gregor, willing him to privacy.

"How about the three of us step inside my office?" Gregor asked diplomatically.

Jonas's jaw ticked, but he said, "Yes. That's a good idea."

Jonas took my hand, helping me to my feet, and I stumbled.

"This will have to be quick."

The concern in his voice had me looking up at him. His face was stricken and my heart stuttered. He placed his hand on the small of my back, and I looked around us. The whole floor was now crowded around. Jonas followed my gaze and came to the realization this wasn't the place to cause a scene. He straightened, putting his mask back in place along with his body language that exuded confidence.

"Yes, of course," Gregor said.

We walked into his office and Gregor closed the

door.

Jonas guided me to take one of the seats. He removed a pile of books from the second seat before he sat down, resting his hand possessively on my knee. My head turned to Gregor, eyes wide with questions, the first of which being whether he would let his hatred of Jonas turn into a fight here.

He shook his head and winked at me. "It's fine, Lily. I just want to speak with him," Gregor said assuredly.

I let go of the breath I had been holding.

Gregor turned his attention to Jonas. "Dani informed you about—"

"Declan. Yes, she did. I just learned about it today,"

The hurt and disappointment in his voice had me hunching in my seat. His hand touched my back and pressed in, feeling along my ribs. He cursed under his breath.

"I want you to know that Lily is very important to me as an assistant and as a friend. I don't want her to be hurt in any way. So tell me what your intention is," Gregor said.

"Gregor…." My voice cracked. Risking Jonas as a client was not something Gregor could, or should, do. For the sake of Arch, he needed this win. *I ruin everything I touch.* "I'm sorry, Jonas. Gregor didn't mean that. He…."

"Meant every word of it … and that's okay." Jonas tilted his head. "Gregor has his feelings about the past, and I have mine. But it's important for him to know that my intention for you is between us."

Gregor jutted his chin, his eyes shifted to me. "Is this what you want to do, Lily?"

I licked my lips. "Yes," I whispered.

"Okay, but if you need me to come get you...."

"You most certainly will not," Jonas said.

I frowned. "Stop, please." I turned to Jonas. "I have work. I can meet you after...."

"No. You're leaving with me now," Jonas said.

Gregor held up his hand. "You can go. I'll send you some of the files. Marketing said you could do some edits for them as extra work."

"She won't be doing extra work," Jonas said and folded his arms. "You obviously know Lily's situation is serious. So, are we done?"

I glared at him. I didn't expect Jonas's rudeness, nor did I want him to mess up my job.

"I most certainly will...." I swiped my forehead.

Gregor gazed at me and the corners of his mouth turned down. "No, Lily. I agree with," he paused and sighed. "I agree with Jonas. I think you leaving right now is ... for the best."

He turned his sad eyes to me. I didn't understand and gave him a questioning look.

"I can stay. I don't want to leave you without help."

"It's okay, Lily. Mark can fill in for a while." Gregor lips curved. "You should go now. We'll talk about it later. I'll call and check-up on you."

Jonas immediately stood up. He shook Gregor's

hand then took mine, walking us to the door. I looked over my shoulder. My eyes connected to Gregor's and he winked.

"It's okay, Lily. Go with Jonas."

I gave him a weak smile. "Thank you."

I closed the door behind us, leaving me at Jonas's side. Jonas being a renowned businessman, as well as a potential celebrity client—not to mention the fact that he was gorgeous—had created a stir around our corner of the building. The crowd had doubled since we'd gone into Gregor's office. People were milling around, acting as if they were busy, and all the while sneaking as many peeks as they could.

Jonas surprised me by wrapping his arms around me in a tight hug. "I'll save the scolding for later."

Just then, my phone sounded, alerting me to a new message. Was it Declan? My heartbeat picked up. What was I doing? I couldn't go. I needed him to understand.

"I wish I could go with you, but I can't. You don't know what's going on…."

He swept me up off my feet. "I'll carry you out of here."

"Put me down," I protested, looking around in a panic. The eyes of all of my co-workers were on us. "Why are you behaving this way? Everyone is staring at us."

"I don't give a damn. You lied and deceived me for weeks. I gave you time, and I can't give you anymore. I won't give you any more," Jonas said with irritation in his voice. He eased me back to my feet and tucked me close to his side, as if he feared breaking contact. "You're coming with me walking or over my shoulder. Your choice, but we leave now together."

My heart skipped a beat as I stared at him. The feelings that I had for him engulfed me. He moved us to my desk and unplugged my phone with his free hand. A tear slid down my cheek and I let out a whimper. He turned around and cupped my face before kissing my forehead.

"Everything will be fine."

I stared at him in awe as he picked up my handbag and put it on his shoulder. "Gregor and Arch need your meeting."

"We'll discuss Arch and everything else later. Right now, we need to get you better," he said.

I curled my chin under. I wanted Jonas to see me as strong, but he saw me as weak.

"There is no 'we.' *I* take care of me. I don't want you to take care of me."

Jonas flattened his mouth into a line and shrugged. "You'll adjust."

He took my hand and started walking, forcing me to follow him. He kept his hand tight as we went down the escalator. Ignoring the looks from the Arch staff that recognized him, he moved us forward and out of the building.

Once in front of his car, David took my things from Jonas. The look he gave me brought tears to my eyes. His gaze was so full of concern I didn't even understand it. I climbed inside with Jonas seated next to me.

"Your doctor's address?" Jonas's tone was clipped.

I wanted to argue with him, but I could see from his expression he was hurting, and I ached for my part in it. So I told him.

"Dr. Steinman on Park and 52nd," I said. "But why do we need to go there?"

He didn't answer, just took out his phone. "Jessie. Crane, here. Call Dr. Steinman's practice, and get an emergency appointment for Lily Salomé. We're on our way there." He repeated the address.

I pursed my lips. "I don't see any reason I need to bother my doctor. He has a busy practice. I could be waiting to see him for hours." Then another thought occurred to me. "What about your work?"

"That's for me to worry about," Jonas said. "He will see you today."

He was a warrior in the business world now. I imagined him charging in and ordering Dr. Steinman to see me, and stifled a laugh. Dr. Steinman was ex-marine and no nonsense. It would be quite a show.

He told David the address and we sat in silence on the drive to Dr. Steinman's office. Jonas's demeanor left no room for negotiation, and his grip on my hand left no room for escape.

I looked at him out of the corner of my eye. "Jonas. We need to talk."

"Oh, that's one thing you don't have to worry about, Lily. We will talk and you will tell me everything," he said, enunciating every word with conviction.

My heart skipped a beat. Jonas going all commando actually turned me on, despite all that was going on around me. The purse of his full lips was also undeniably sexy.

I turned my head to hide my toothy grin while Jonas brooded next to me. Once I collected myself, I said quietly, "I'm happy to see you."

"Come here," Jonas said in a low rumble. I moved a little, and he took that as an agreement to take me in his lap and hold me there.

Jonas had taken me. I closed my eyes and relaxed in his arms, allowing myself to enjoy this dream.

CHAPTER SIXTEEN

"**S**O, WHAT AM I supposed to tell them?" I asked as we walked inside the doors of the building housing Dr. Steinman's office.

Jonas's eyes dulled as he tightened his grip on my hand. "My assistant told them you're ill. They'll check out the rest," he said assuredly.

I exhaled and walked inside the medium-sized doctor's office. It had all the staples of most doctors' offices, peach-colored décor, and framed posters of happy, healthy people doing the right thing hung on the walls. The space was complete with a fish tank gurgling in the corner. The small seating area had a coffee table littered with magazines and a couple of people seated in the cushioned seats. One looked okay, while the other looked like they were a minute from barfing. Note to self, sit as far as possible away from that person.

We walked up to check in at the built-in desk with a computer and a smiling young lady eyeing Jonas.

"Insurance card," she said to Jonas.

I scrambled in my purse for the card, and he handed

it to her giving her one of his winning smiles, to my annoyance. He placed his hand on my back once we were finished, oblivious or ignoring my irritation. Part of me was sure he was upset with me, though.

We went to sit in the waiting area for my emergency appointment. I kept glancing at Jonas, expecting him to leave or use his phone. But he didn't do either. He sat there and held my hand, as if he had all the time in the world for me. I didn't have words for the feelings aroused in me.

After a little over an hour, a slender woman with honey smooth skin and pressed hair dressed in a brightly colored uniform opened the door and called out my name. I stood up, and was surprised when Jonas stood to accompany me.

"Mr…?" the nurse asked, clearly surprised herself.

"Crane, her fiancé," Jonas said with a completely straight face.

My mouth dropped, but I just nodded. She didn't press the matter, instead escorting us into an examination room.

"You're not feeling well, Lily?" the nurse asked as she perused my chart.

I looked at Jonas, who took a seat in one of the small chairs next to the examination tables.

"No," was all I could think to say.

"How about I take your vitals? Dr. Steinman will be with you shortly," she said.

I slipped off my shoes out of normal habit when approaching a scale.

"Step on the scale and I'll take your weight and blood pressure," the nurse said, as if I didn't understand the word "vitals."

I climbed on the scale. My pulse sped up as we looked at the reading. My jaw unhinged. I didn't weigh myself much, as I usually found the numbers depressing. This time the number was much less than what I anticipated. I thought back over the last few months and my reduced calorie diet, exercise, half eaten meals, and lack of appetite.

The nurse lowered her eyes to the clipboard. "You're a bit underweight. Please have a seat and I'll check your blood pressure." I stepped down from the scale and sat down on the examination table. She put down her chart and wrapped the gauge around my arm. "Your blood pressure is a little low, too, sweetheart."

She checked it twice digitally, then switched to manual, using her wrist and watch. Jonas grunted.

"Hmm. I'll have Dr. Steinman perform a second check. Or an EKG. You say you're not feeling well?" she asked again.

I met Jonas's eyes. They were watery.

I stared down at my feet. "I've been really tired lately … lethargic."

"Okay. You can put on a gown, and Dr. Steinman will check you over," the nurse said, pulling out a gown from a hidden drawer under the exam table. "Take off everything but your panties."

She eyed Jonas, then left the small room.

I started unbuttoning my suit jacket and hesitated, a blush creeping up my face. I could feel his stare on me.

"Would you turn away?"

"No," Jonas said.

I frowned. "No?" I repeated.

"We are certainly past this, Lily," Jonas said, crossing his arms.

I turned away from him and eased off my suit, jacket, and skirt. When I got down to my bra and panties, he let out an audible gasp. I dropped my chin. He was repulsed by me, just like Declan had said. I quickly put on the gown then I sat and put my head in my hands. Jonas was suddenly there, his arms around me.

"I'm really fine," I promised. "I didn't realize I had dropped that much. I'll eat more."

"You will," he said with conviction in his voice.

He pressed a kiss to the side of my head before Dr. Steinman walked into the room. Dr. Steinman's military precision, pewter-colored crew cut was tight to his scalp. The style matched his pristine white coat and shirt and perfectly cut navy slacks. He kind of reminded me of that marine leader with the scar in the movie *Avatar* that I had a bit of a crush on. His steely gaze took us in.

"Should I come back?" he mused with a brow raised.

Jonas undeterred by his presence took his time letting me go.

"He's my … fiancé," I lied in explanation.

Dr. Steinman turned to Jonas.

"Yes, that's right," Jonas said with an air of authority as he took a seat.

"Fine."

Dr. Steinman went straight to work, checking my thyroid, heartbeat, back, and stomach.

He sighed. "Lily. You're underweight. Any more weight loss would be a danger to your health. You're at risk of heart failure with your low blood pressure, not to mention, septic shock and neurological disorders. I'm taking your blood and testing for iron deficiency today."

I touched my full hips. "I ... My body is still...."

I couldn't find the words for what I wanted to say, but it wasn't like I was super skinny or anything. I still had some curves. It hadn't even occurred to me that where I was might be unhealthy. So many women were so much thinner than me.

He pressed his lips together, somehow understanding what I was thinking. "Your body's natural frame is never going to be waif thin. Some people are naturally thin and healthy. You're not. Perhaps a nutritionist or counselor would be necessary?"

"She'll go to both," Jonas interjected. "We'll need the referrals."

"Good," Dr. Steinman said. Both men seemed to be ignoring me. "She can return in two weeks. We'll call with the blood test results. I suspect iron deficiency, but I'll check everything." He finally looked at me. "Are you tired all the time? How's the sleep and stress?"

"She was physically attacked." The anger and hurt in

Jonas's voice shamed me. "You can see the dark circles and puffiness around her eyes. She's not sleeping."

My shoulders slumped.

Dr. Steinman smiled at Jonas. "Thanks for answering for her. Let's hear what she has to say for herself."

Jonas lifted his chin.

I grimaced. "I've been unable to sleep. I take sleeping pills occasionally. As for stress…." I thought about Declan and glanced at Jonas. "I have been under stress."

"Then, Lily, this is your warning," Dr. Steinman said. "It's you that needs to start helping yourself, or give in and go for hospitalization and have us insert a feeding tube. Hopefully that won't get infected and cause other long term problems. Your other option is succumbing to possible debilitating illnesses or death."

"That's not going to happen," Jonas spoke up.

I grimaced and crossed my arms. "That's harsh."

"I'm here to help my patients get better," Dr. Steinman said. "So, if it scares you into health, I did my job. I don't want you collapsing at work so I will write a request for stress leave that you can submit to your Human Resources Department. I'll leave it in front with the counseling referral." He turned to Jonas. "You're her fiancé, so take care of her. I'm not giving her medication. Healthy meals, slow weight gain. She should have warm milk, massages, absolutely no stress and therapy."

"I will take care of her," Jonas said. "And we'll be here for the next appointment. Thank you."

My eyes widened in surprise at Jonas's assurance. He

couldn't promise to be here in two weeks. He had work.

Dr. Steinman turned back to me. "See you in two weeks, Lily."

He shook Jonas's hand then left.

I turned back and quickly put on my clothing. "Jonas. You can't be here."

"Oh, Lily, I can be wherever I want," Jonas said, not to just for me, but also himself.

He pulled out his phone and began texting someone. When I was changed, he took my hand. We walked out to the front desk and waited a few minutes to collect the referrals before leaving the office.

Once we were seated in the car, Jonas immediately reached for me. I didn't resist as he placed me in his lap. I needed the comfort.

"David. We'll stop in Jersey City. Then, back to the Waldorf hotel," Jonas said.

I hid my face in case he saw my disappointment. We were right back into the same routine. He'd wine, dine, and leave. Still I snuggled against him. And, for the first time in weeks, I slept soundly.

CHAPTER SEVENTEEN

I COULD FEEL his breath on my ear. His nose brushed against me, rousing me from my sleep.

"We're here."

I opened my eyes, looking past him out the windows, and saw my apartment building. My heart sunk. The scene of the crime. My Hell.

"Something wrong?" Jonas asked, tilting my head up to him.

My brows furrowed. Yeah, something was wrong, and it was the gorgeous, unavailable man holding me. I moved off his lap and onto the seat next to him. I had been so enraptured by having Jonas here that I had completely failed to remember what Dani had said about Melissa. He was seeing her now. But she couldn't give him what he needed, a small voice in the back of my head reminded me.

"What are you thinking?" Jonas asked.

I looked up and scowled at him.

He gave me a look with equal irritation and added the quip, "An honest answer."

That took the wind out of my sails, and my scowl became more of a frown. "You deserve an honest answer. So I was thinking that here you are, cuddling me. But you're with Melissa."

Jonas stared at me and didn't answer. That was answer enough for me.

I lifted my chin. "Thank you for attending my appointment. I'm sorry for any inconvenience I may have caused you. I didn't realize I had loss weight and ... well, I'm home now so ... see you," I babbled.

Jonas crossed his arms. We sat for a moment in silence.

He then said, "My turn?"

I shrugged.

"You removed yourself from my life. So I don't think it would be fair to expect me not to try to move on. What do you think?" he asked bluntly.

I breathed through the truth and pain of his words. I covered my mouth as a wave of nausea went through me at the thought of Jonas with someone else. I had been naïve, of course. And in truth, I had never expected him to wait for me. My head fell forward.

"So what are you doing here? You should go." My voice broke.

Jonas's mouth tightened. "You want me to go?"

I shook my head. "Do you want to stay?" I whispered.

My bottom lip trembled.

"Yes, Lily, I want to stay."

Jonas took my hand and brushed his lips against the back of it. I would have given anything for Jonas to assure me of his intentions, but he didn't. Instead, he helped me out of the car while David handed me my keys from the pocket of my handbag to unlock the door. I saved the protest on my lips as I quickly realized neither one of them was going to listen to me. Not to mention, the tick in Jonas's jaw let me know he was still upset with me.

I tried to push my brain on the subject, but found it all too exhausting. In fact, I was practically dead on my feet. This must have come across as it took me a minute to unlock the front door once we reached my apartment. Jonas eventually took the keys away and unlocked it himself. My eyes scanned the place for anything embarrassing, as I hadn't been expecting company. My unmade couch bed was the first thing I went to correct, walking over and folding my pillows and the blanket I had left out.

"You're place looks different," Jonas said.

He eyed the empty places where the lamps used to be. I hadn't moved the furniture around to fill in the spaces.

"My roommate, Natasha, moved out a while ago."

The sound of my cabinets being opened and closed had me looking at the kitchen. Jonas was looking inside of them.

"What about your lease?" he asked as he opened my refrigerator and pursed his lips. "All I see is yogurt and water here. What did you eat for breakfast?"

My scalp felt damp. I walked over to the thermostat along the wall and checked the temperature. It was off, and for the loft that usually meant cold. I tried to recall everything that had happened during the day. When did I last eat?

"A salad for lunch. I'll call and see if I can get a delivery tonight. I'm fine now. Maybe I'll take a nap. Or do you want to talk?" I rambled as I squirmed, watching him look in every cabinet and even at my garbage. "What are you doing?" I asked with annoyance.

I already knew he was searching for food. He didn't trust I would give him a straight answer.

"I haven't gone shopping yet. I usually eat at work anyway," I said, offering an explanation.

Jonas reached inside the refrigerator. He took out the four cups of fat free yogurt, all my least favorites left, and a spoon.

"You're tired. Go to the bedroom, sit on the bed and wait for me. You'll eat these and take a nap before we leave for the hotel. We'll get dinner in a couple of hours. Oh, and you haven't answered on your lease."

I crossed my arms and planted my feet. I didn't move, but answered him, "A couple of months. I'm looking for a studio here, Brooklyn and Queens. But is that what this is?" I gestured between us. "You're ordering me around like a child."

Jonas gave me a look that said "how could you ask me that?" With all my lies and deception, I couldn't blame him for being upset, but that still didn't explain his actions.

I was frustrated, but the hurt in his eyes made me respond, "I'm sorry about … everything."

"Everything? This doesn't settle everything. You'll tell me everything," Jonas said in a crisp tone.

I shuffled on my feet. "I don't expect you to understand."

He closed his eyes and took in a deep breath. "Dr. Steinman said not to stress you. So I apologize if my anger is upsetting you, but I just learned that motherfucking piece of shit ex of yours beat you. And you told Ian and Dani, not me."

The hurt and disappointment in his voice cut into me. I casted my eyes down as guilt encompassed me.

Jonas ran his hand through his hair. "I'm trying, Lily. But what I need from you right now is to do as you're told."

"I most certainly will not," I said petulantly.

The effect would have gone over better if I hadn't yawned.

"Do you need me to carry you? I will."

He suppressed the grin on his face.

I leaned against the couch and looked away. That was all the time it took for Jonas to cross the room and swoop me up like a damsel in distress. There were no words I would be able to say to change his mind about what he intended for me. I relaxed into his hold. He pressed his lips to my forehead then carried me across the room, paying no mind to his black suit, which I crushed and creased against him.

My bedroom. I let out the breath I was holding once I saw the lights were off. Declan hadn't managed to come back inside, but his being there at all still poisoned my view of the room.

"Eat and nap," Jonas said, placing me down on the bed.

I rolled my eyes, but gave a little nod. "You gonna baby me?" I whispered.

Jonas finally smiled back at me. "I suppose I am."

Everything was fuzzy, as he fed me spoon after spoon of yogurt.

"Don't taste good together," I believe I mumbled.

"You'll eat more soon. Rest now," he said.

I began to drift off. I was warm. Too warm. I tugged off my suit before falling into a dream.

"I love you, Jonas."
"I … love you, darling."
"I need you. Please stay."
"I'm not going anywhere, my little tiger."

"I don't give a damn. You will listen to me. Declan. Declan Gilroy. Find everything you can. That fucker won't have two nickels to rub together to get a defense attorney."

My eyes popped open and I screamed, "You can't!" My bedroom door flew open and Jonas rushed inside, his phone in hand.

Jonas stared at me. I paused under the weight of his glare and looked down. I was no longer dressed in my suit. No bra. Just a tank top. I didn't remember putting on panties. Did Jonas change me? I timidly gazed back at him and my answer was there. Yes, he did.

I shook my head to return my focus to the issue at hand. Jonas was going after Declan and he couldn't. "You can't. You're going to make everything worse."

"I'll call you back. No. Go ahead." Jonas's mouth was in a firm line. He placed his phone inside his suit jacket. "Explain."

"Are you going to listen?" I asked my voice elevated. "This is why I didn't want you to know. This is why I kept this from you." I swallowed. "The police arrested Declan at his business. He's furious. And he took...."

Jonas's facial expression went lethal.

I was bawling now. Jonas sat down next to me and took my face in his hands.

"Tell me. Right now," he commanded.

"I can't. Please. It'll make it worse." I tried to shake my head in his hands. "Please understand."

"No. I don't understand. I'm not calling anyone off. You tell me right now what you're hiding," Jonas demanded.

"He came in and took my book and ripped some of my photos. He has more photos."

My skin heated and Jonas's face turned menacing. He started to shake.

"He'll return the book. And he'll stop with the photos," I pleaded. "He's just upset. Don't ruin his life. Please. Jonas. Don't do anything. Give him a chance to get himself together. I'm fine now. So please."

"No you're not, but you will be. I promise you," he whispered.

He pulled me into his arms and held me His comfort and care was what I longed for, and I took it, molding myself against him. I couldn't get close enough, and he patiently let me. He was a mountain of strength, and I was broken, but in his arms, I came together.

CHAPTER EIGHTEEN

I WOKE WITH a start outside of the Waldorf. I hadn't realized I'd fallen asleep again. I kept my eyes closed for a few extra moments and inhaled, taking in Jonas's scent and the warmth of his body. I peered through my lashes and made out his expression from the light coming through the window. His beautifully sculpted face was set in stone. My heart lurched. I had become a disruption in his order. He'd spent most of the afternoon and part of the evening with me. From our short time together and public knowledge of him, I knew Jonas wasn't the type to miss meetings or work. Yet he had managed to miss both because of me. He had put up with a doctor's office and mini breakdowns over my ex. Hell, he'd even changed me, fed me, and got me in the car once I had settled down, not allowing me to pack a thing.

"You'll get everything you wanted," Dani had said.

Was this what I wanted? Jonas babying me?

I shifted, ready and not ready for him to release me. His full lips brushed against my forehead, and my heart fluttered as I imagined him holding me all night. But I couldn't do that to him or me. My weakness was only making my dreams of being with him further away. Where I was right now, I doubted I would even make a companion for him. I didn't have to worry about that, though. I had become a landmine of issues. Hell, I was crazy high maintenance. Most of all, Jonas didn't belong to me. I was borrowing him from Melissa.

"What are you thinking?" Jonas asked, a frown marring his gorgeous profile.

"Nothing," I mumbled. Then quickly answered "Melissa" before he pressed me for a real answer.

His brows returned to normal and he nodded. This time I didn't look for the reassurance I needed, instead I simply climbed out of the car. I looked around at the high-classed clientele, all dressed in the latest and greatest designer wear.

And what was I wearing? A fleece with a tank top hanging out the bottom, sweatpants, and socks with ballet flats thanks to our quick exit from my apartment after our conversation about Declan. My hair was still nice from Dee's magic, but still, I looked a mess. I dropped my head in embarrassment. That was when I felt Jonas's arm settle around my shoulder, tucking me against his body.

I braced myself for what I'd find when I glanced up at him. Surely there would be a hint of embarrassment at being seen with me at his lustrous second home, dressed in such contrast to his dark designer suit. However, what

I found instead was his air of confidence that defied my appearance and dared challenging. This became even more evident with the manner in which all responded to him as the bell person collected my things from David, and led us through the hotel and up to his suite.

My heart swelled. God, I loved this man. He caught my love struck gaze, and winked at me.

"Let's go," Jonas whispered.

We walked through the lobby like rock stars. Well, I was the lucky groupie and Jonas was the eye catching lead singer. All adoration pointed to him, which he acted oblivious to as we trouped up to his suite with the bell person rolling his briefcase and the trolley bag I didn't recall packing.

Once inside his suite, Jonas still hadn't released me. Instead, he reached with one hand inside his coat and tipped the bag person. He walked us over to the phone once the door was closed.

"Jonas, I'm not feeling dizzy anymore. You can release me."

I giggled at the oddity of us joined at the hip. He ignored me and continued his call. I realized then that he was a quiet storm next to me.

"Steak, roast chicken. Salad, and fruit cups." Once he completed the order, he announced, "We'll have dinner and you'll go to sleep. You can go take a bath now. Everything else, we'll discuss tomorrow."

I pressed my hand to my stomach. "Don't you think we should talk? I'm not hungry—"

"I have work and phone calls to make right now. So just do as I say." His tone was low and authoritative.

"Again with that? I'm not a child."

I twisted away from him and he allowed me to go.

Jonas scoffed. "But you want to argue like one? I'll bathe, feed, and put you to bed."

My mind imagined Jonas's hands all over my body, and a goofy grin spread across my face. He should have known that wasn't going to motivate me. I was about to challenge him, but I saw the tiredness on his face.

"Were you travelling today?" I asked.

"No. I have been in town for a few days. I've just had a lot come up with work, and Paul had me out with him at a rock concert last night."

He took on that look of pride and pleasure he had when he talked about his son.

"You must be tired," I said. "And you're probably behind with work. You spent the whole day with me...."

A crease appeared on his cheek. "After all you've been through, and you're worried about me? Don't worry. I'm fine."

"Alright, I won't fight. I'll follow your orders. Mr. Crane, sir," I said and jokingly saluted him.

He stared at me, then walked over and kissed my forehead, which was becoming his go-to spot. I didn't love it.

"Good," he said. "If you need help, just call out."

I turned my head so he wouldn't see the mischief in my expression. "I don't have anything to wear."

"I packed a T-shirt you can sleep in," Jonas said, his hands on my shoulders moved me toward the bathroom.

"Okay. I'm going. Do I smell or something?" I joked, sniffing myself.

"No, but Dr. Steinman said warm baths and relaxation, and I agree," he said.

I walked inside the bathroom and started to undress. I could feel Jonas's gaze, but when I turned around, he turned and walked out.

"I'm right outside," he called over his shoulder.

My old records had a new insult. Now my weight loss repulsed him. I walked over to the tub and started filling it, climbing in when the water reached mid-way. I cleaned up, washing and moisturizing my face. Upon getting out, I pulled on a tank top and pants, easing the door open and walking out. Jonas was facing towards the windows. He had removed his suit jacket and was still in his shirt and slacks, his stance stoic.

"No. Don't come. Yes, I do. It is." He turned to look at me and motioned towards the dining table. "Yes. If that's what you want to do. Good night."

He hung up the phone and pushed his hands through his hair.

I hesitated. "Is everything okay?" I asked.

"Yes. Well, it will be," he said and walked over to the table and held my seat out.

I sat down and he took the seat next to me. Everything smelled wonderful. I eyed the roast chicken, Mediterranean vegetables, and rice pilaf on my plate. I tried to remember what I had last eaten before the yogurt, but nothing sprang to mind.

Jonas spoke, drawing me out of my thoughts. "Let's enjoy our dinner."

He watched me as I lifted a fork full of rice and ate it. Only then did he visibly ease.

"No quotes, Mr. Crane?" I asked.

He smiled wistfully. "Not tonight, Ms. Salomé." He ate his grilled steak and tabbouleh salad, in between sending his fork over to me to try. "Just a bite."

I rolled my eyes. "You're going to make my stomach explode."

He didn't laugh, and we continued to eat in silence. I took a few more bites of my own and felt full.

"How about a few bites of the fruit cup?" Jonas asked.

I shook my head. "I'm honestly stuffed. I'd rather not."

Tension rose between us. My stomach knotted. I was at war with myself in wanting to please him, but at the same time getting him to believe me. I glanced at him and could still see the tension in his jaw as he stared at my plate.

"Please don't get upset," I mumbled.

"Don't tell me how to feel," Jonas said. Then he took a breath, placing his hand over mine. "I won't over-whelm you tonight, but I'm here."

My lips parted. I wanted to ask for how long, but feared his answer. "You don't have to do this. Why are you?"

"Because you are my friend, first and foremost. And you need me." Jonas squeezed my hand. "Now, I want you to sleep."

I stifled a yawn as I said, "I'm not that tired."

Jonas reached out and stroked my hair. "Yes, you are," he said softly.

My pulse sped up. "Are you joining me?"

He looked away. "No. I have work. I'll sleep later."

I plastered on a smile. "I didn't think the next time I saw you would turn out like this. I'm sorry for lying to you. Thank you for … everything."

He hugged me to him. "I just wish I had known."

He took my hand and walked me back to the bed. Once I was under the duvet, he cupped the side of my face.

I stared into his eyes. *Please touch me.* "Thank you."

"Get some rest."

He kissed the end of my nose and let go. I sighed and watched him climb off the bed and leave the bedroom.

My mind started to race, blocking my exhaustion. I removed my T-shirt and dumped it on the side of the bed, but left my underwear on and curled up on my side.

"Lily."

Jonas came back. He had removed his work shirt and was now in a T-shirt and slacks. He climbed on top of the covers as he stretched out next to me.

"Work can wait."

He stroked my hair, but didn't move to climb under

the covers to join me. My vision blurred as I relaxed into the soothing, rhythmic strokes of his hand petting me.

"I'd like to have a look under that skirt, lay back," he ordered.

My pulse sped up again as heat rose in my body.

"Jonas," I whined.

He slid his hand higher. He shook his head as he reached my skirt and tugged down my tights and panties.

"Thigh highs and no panties tonight. I want to have access whenever I want to touch you."

I squirmed and took in a short breath.

"Breathe, Lily."

He gazed at me and we took in a few breaths together, until we synced. He opened my thighs and dropped his gaze.

"You're beautiful and aroused. I can't leave you like this. But, I'll give you a choice."

He pushed a finger inside me.

"Oh, God. Please," I said breathy.

"My hand," Jonas whispered.

He leaned down and swirled his tongue around my clit. "My tongue or…."

"Jonas. Please," I begged as my pulse pounded in my throat.

He unzipped his trousers and pulled out his cock, rubbing it against my slick sex. "My cock."

Yes. Jonas.

"Lily."

"Your cock. Please," I cried out.

"Lily," he chuckled.

I woke with a start. *Jonas.* My skin was on fire as my awareness came fully back to me. Shit. I froze. Light shone behind my eyelids, which were now tightly squeezed shut as awareness of my place and actions came back to me. I loosened my hand, still in my panties, slick with my arousal. Why me?

The sound of our breathing filled a few minutes, as I continued to lay there stuck between the bliss of my dream and the real mortification before me. I realized I hadn't waxed, and that thought alone further fueled my discomfort. That and the realization Jonas had changed my clothing earlier. He'd probably seen. My skin warmed all the more.

"Lily. It's okay," Jonas said softly.

I started to remove my hand, but I felt Jonas's hand on my wrist.

"Don't."

His breathing was heavier.

My eyes opened and my breath hitched as I found him sitting up next to me, looking edible in just his briefs. His gaze burned into my hand where it still rested inside my panties. I squirmed as heat flooded my body and my pulse sped up.

Jonas's eyes moved to mine and they were almost black. His jaw was taught. He was right on the edge of need himself. He moved his hand to the top of my panties and pressed a finger between mine. He took in a sharp breath as he felt the soaked fabric. I moaned loudly and my hips lifted. That was all he needed.

"Finish now," Jonas growled out.

Our eyes met, and our connection crackled between us.

My breath was ragged as I shifted against his finger, willing him to continue, as I rubbed my clit under his apt gaze. He shifted closer and I caught sight of his erection, tenting the front of his briefs. I reached out and tugged at the top of them. I wanted him inside me more than I wanted my next breath.

Jonas gripped my hand, stopping me. "Fuck."

He grunted and closed his eyes, his fingers slipping behind my panties and stroking my clit. That was all I needed. I gapped my legs wider. My hand moved out of the way and gripped the sheets as he continued to stroke my pussy with his finger.

"We shouldn't. You're sick," he said hoarsely, but neither of us wanted him to stop, and he didn't.

Pushing a finger in and curving it up, he honed in on my G-spot. My eyes rolling in my head, I cried out. I had already been on the edge of climax before he'd started fucking me with his fingers. He added another, sliding them in and out of my pussy. The slick, wet sound filled my ears as I moaned loudly, trying to hold back my climax.

"Was I doing this in your dream? Tell me," he said in a low tone. "Was I fucking you?"

His words broke me apart, and I shuddered under his fingers as I climaxed.

My body knew him and wanted more. I feared he would stop, but was pleased when I watched him pull off his briefs and grip his long, thick cock in his hand. The sight of him naked before me had me hot with desire for him again, like he hadn't just sated me moments before. It couldn't be helped. His body was a work of art. He was all lean muscles and tanned skin. The smooth hair on his chest lead down to his fully engorged cock. Beads of pre-cum glistened on the tip, making my mouth water.

I leaned over and swiped my tongue over the head to taste him. He let out a groan. I moved my mouth to slide him in further. Fuck. He was hard as steel. He needed this. My jaw struggled to accommodate him, and I fought hard not to choke, fearing he would make me stop if I did. He was panting hard, though. He didn't have the will to stop this.

I wickedly took full advantage and closed my mouth around his shaft as I slid him to the back of my throat. Jonas's eyes were tightly shut, his body tensed. His hips rocked a little, letting me know he had some control left, but needed for me to go faster. I wrapped a hand around his shaft and cupped his balls. I fell into his rhythm as I stroked him, continuing to lick and suck his cock. His balls started to tighten in my hand. He was close. I sucked and stroked faster.

"Lily, Oh!" he cried out.

He thrust fast and exploded in my mouth. I only sucked harder as I swallowed down every drop. Yes. He was mine.

As Jonas came down, he touched my face and I let him go. He stared at me and I grinned up at him, feeling all the more wanted for having made him cave on his own resolve. But to my horror, I watched as his desire changed to empathy, his eyes cascading over my body.

"Oh, Lily. I shouldn't ... We shouldn't have."

"You're no longer attracted to me," I said in a small voice and moved to my side.

He sighed. "I think I proved that I am, and you know that. But you are very thin, and I'm worried about you."

I knew his words came from a place of caring, but I was upset he had ruined what we just experienced. He moved my hair and kissed the back of my neck. His lips moved down my shoulder as his hand reached around and under my panties to cup my mound. His touch awakened my arousal again as his fingers rubbed me there. I could feel his cock coming alive against my back again, further proving his point. He was sexually attracted to me. I knew he was trying to comfort me now, but I wanted so much more.

"Fuck me," I whispered.

"I would take you too rough. I don't want to hurt you," he said.

I squeezed my eyes shut as I panted and moved against his hand. "I'm ... thin, not fragile."

I rasped a plea on my lips as he ground against me. Our breathing became staggered. His touch only made us hotter, taking us further from sleep.

Must I beg? I let out a frustrated whimper as I pressed back into him. Fine.

"Please," I whispered again.

Jonas removed his hand and turned over on his back. Our pants filled the night.

"Only you, Lily. Turning me into a lover and not a fucker," he growled out.

I let out a snort in frustration. What did he mean by that? From where I laid, there was no fucking going on here.

"Take off your panties," he said in a guttural tone.

I hooked the side of my panties, pulled them down and kicked them off.

"Straddle me," he commanded. I straddled his waist and reached behind me to take his cock, but he grabbed my ass and moved me up. "My face."

He meant his mouth, but I didn't protest. Something was off with him. And I knew there was something I was supposed to remember, but the minute his mouth sealed on my pussy, all thoughts left me as bliss took hold of me. His tongue swirled inside me.

"Oh, Jonas. God," I praised as he devoured me.

He flicked, lapped and sucked my pussy, rolling one climax on top of another. I tried to move away, seeking relief from the intensity, but he grunted and held me tight as he kept on eating me with a vengeance. Was he punishing me? The thought escaped as I cried out to him, waves of pleasure overwhelming me.

"Jonas," I groaned and moaned as I convulsed and came again, vibrating with the force of the moment. "Just fuck me," I finally hissed.

He paused. *That* was his line.

"Fuck …Fuck it," he bit out.

He let me go and moved me down, his cock slipping inside me in one ecstatic, long glide. We moaned and stayed still, joined together. His eyes opened and I was sure my heart swelled in my chest, as our connection sealed between us. This was perfect. This was where he belonged.

Gripping my hips, he moved me up and down his cock at a slow and gentle pace. I placed my hand on his clenched, muscled abs, as the sensations coursed through my body, building us to release. I looked down at Jonas's face and my heart flipped at his bliss and struggle for control as he sought not to hurt me. He lifted up his hips between light touches on my breasts.

Just then, his body tensed and he called out my name as he released beneath me, spilling hot inside me, bringing on another orgasm from within my walls. I echoed his name as my sex spasmed around him, milking him. My body shook as ecstasy blanketed me. We stayed that way for a few minutes, and then he lifted me off with ease and I stretched out on my back. I turned over and caught a bit of a scowl on his mouth, though his eyes were heavily lidded as he turned off the light.

"Rest," he commanded. He pulled me to his side like a caveman to spoon me. "Go to sleep," he said, just in case I didn't remember what "rest" meant.

If I wasn't so passionately spent, I would have been upset at his sudden change of attitude and behavior, but then it hit me. I was categorically his friend now, and as a personal rule of his, he wasn't intimate with friends. He was supposed to be with Melissa.

Borrowing his words, fuck it.

CHAPTER NINETEEN

A WARM HAND on my shoulder broke through the barrier of my sleep.

"I'm sorry to wake you up, but it's close to eight and I need you to have breakfast before I leave."

His breath tickled my ear, and I cracked a smile, which must be why he pressed in with his lips.

"Eight?" I croaked.

My eyes fluttered open to find Jonas leaning over me at the side of the bed. His hand lingered and warmed my shoulder as it rubbed down my arm. A thrill went through me. He couldn't stop touching me. My body craved more.

I looked past him to the bright light of day shining through the gap in the heavy embroidered curtains in his hotel bedroom. When I rolled over onto my back, Jonas made a sound that caused heat to fill my body. His eyes followed my movements as I pulled up the sheet to cover my nipples, which immediately started poking out through the thin layer of fabric. I took in a shallow breath. His hand moved towards me, then detoured to adjust the bulge poking out the front of his dark trousers.

He turned his head. "Last night, I lost … We both lost control."

It was his way of cutting straight to the issue at hand. He was so unlike me in this way, as I would have, of course, preferred to think and process through everything before talking about it.

I licked my lips. "Yes … of course. You're with Melissa."

My voice went up at the end, making this sound more like a question, as if I thought last night meant he would leave her and choose me. That wasn't something I believed, nor did I think it possible. Not after everything that had happened.

I opened my mouth to correct my error, but Jonas spoke first.

"What I'm more concerned about right now is your well-being," he said, not exactly answering my non-question. "I didn't mean to take advantage of you. I mean, you're sick…."

His words hit my heart.

"Nothing happened that I didn't want to happen," I said in a soft voice. I lifted my chin, but could only meet the stubble along his. "I didn't mean to take advantage of you. You've been so helpful to me with the doctor and everything yesterday. I think it was only natural for us to fall back into … In our situation, and with the close proximity…."

I didn't know what the hell I was saying, but Jonas

nodded and said, "True."

He took the "I'm not a jerk for cheating on my current girl with my ex" out I had given to him. Was he cheating? If Melissa was his companion, I supposed not. But I bet she, like me, wouldn't see it that way.

I really didn't want to be naked right now, and so I started searching around for something to put on. Jonas stood and crossed the room, collecting a robe from a chair in the corner and bringing it back to the bed. He held it open for me to put on.

"Let's go have breakfast."

"I'm not…." I let the words die as I met the scowl marring his handsome face. "I'll eat after I shower."

"Now would work better. It will be a few hours before lunch."

The dots from my cluttered mind finally connected. Jonas planned to be my personal food watcher.

"I. Can. Manage," I said, punctuating each word.

Jonas only moved a shoulder and kept his stoic position with the robe, as if he had all day to wait for me. My jaw tightened as I moved with the covers to stand, ignoring the fact that we both knew he had spent part of the night between my thighs with the lights on. I put in an arm and dropped the sheet, then awkwardly put the robe on backwards and quickly closed it up to my neck.

"Stubborn *and* grumpy," he teased.

Before I could react, he swept me off my feet, and I was creasing another one of his pressed shirts as he cradled me.

I narrowed my eyes. "This is going to stop right now. I'm not a baby to be held. I'm not a collie to be petted."

"You like being carried and petted."

Jonas gave me a dark look, which tightened things low on my body. But that couldn't be helped.

"This isn't fucking," he said as he carried me through the bedroom door. "This is giving you what you need."

"What I need is not your concern. Furthermore, I'm not someone that needs their food intake supervised. Carrying me is inappropriate. I mean, we just discussed breaking boundaries last night. So, stop."

He ignored my glare and brought me to the dining table, where he sat me down on the chair before a covered plate and took the seat next to me.

"You practically passed out in front of me yesterday. Do you know I stayed up all night watching you?"

The anguish on his face had me instantly feeling remorse.

I dipped my head. "All I can say is that I'm sorry. I didn't mean to disrupt your sleep or your life. I've been under a lot of ... stress," I said, my voice scratchy.

I didn't want to bring up my situation with Declan again.

I glanced over and noticed that Jonas's eyes had clouded over. "Yes, I know."

The guilt on his face had me reaching out to squeeze his hand. "It's not your fault. This is all my doing."

"No. This is that piece of shit exe's of yours fault." He took in a couple of deep breaths to calm down. "You need support and that includes comforting. It's something I would have given you anyway if you had remained my companion, and I will continue to give you as your friend. Now, eat your breakfast."

My lips parted in protest, but I knew we were both wound too tight after yesterday and last night. So I decidedly removed the lid on the plate before me and found poached eggs, a bagel with cream cheese and salmon. My mind immediately started calculating the caloric intake out of habit, an internal voice telling me I wasn't hungry. As I shifted the food around my plate, I wondered if I really did have a problem.

"Lily," Jonas said my name with slight irritation, calling me back from my thoughts.

I ignored him and took a huge bite out of the salmon and bagel, then peeked at him through my lashes and found him gazing at me intently. A flutter went through my chest, and a small smile snuck to my lips.

"Thank you," Jonas exhaled. "I have a meeting in town."

He mixed the eggs and toast together on his plate and started eating. Back to the real world for Jonas, but not for me. I had been placed on leave.

"I probably should get information to Human Resources and call Gregor—"

"David dropped off the paperwork this morning," Jonas said, interrupting me. "You have an appointment for a massage at the spa in a half hour. Afterwards, a body wax, manicure, and pedicure. By then I should be back for lunch."

My cheeks warmed as I stared at him in disbelief. "I didn't agree to any of that, and I'm not going. I don't need it. I'll take care of the rest when I go home."

"Don't fight with me, Lily. This was your doctor's orders," Jonas said and sipped his coffee.

"Massages, not the rest," I muttered, staring down at my plate.

Maggie crossed my mind, and Gregor's warnings. Even though Jonas had explained his relationship with her, I still didn't want to get caught up in his generosity.

"I don't need to be pampered. I want to function within my means. I know I have problems. I just need some time to think, to plan…."

"And you'll have it," Jonas said. "We still need the results from the blood test, too."

My mouth went dry. "We?"

He reached out and rubbed the frown between my brows. "Yes, 'we.' I'm concerned about you. You need less stress. As far as the rest, I know you like those things." His tone was light.

I pursed my lips and stared at him. I did like the manicure and pedicures, but we both knew the body wax was for him.

"Fine, your body waxing is for me," he finally admitted. "So you'll have it. You're not going—"

Jonas's phone started chiming, interrupting his next declaration. He pulled it out and answered it. I could see the relief on his face as the call ended our second argument of the day, before the day had even started.

"Yes."

He took a small plate and a bagel, a hint of amusement on his face as he eyed my pout. He stood and walked over to the desk where he had set up a workstation, leaving me in my seat to stew. I ate a couple more bites of my bagel and drank the fresh orange juice from the glass pitcher on the table.

What was I going to do?

I turned and looked at Jonas. The pull he had on me flared to life. I wanted every inch of that stubborn, complicated man that was bossing me around, both in and out of the bedroom.

After what I had experienced with Declan, I knew Jonas was motivated by a desire to help, not hurt me. He was my friend, though even that was blurry. Admittedly, we were both responsible for what had complicated us the night before. Neither of us had been able to keep our hands off the other. Still, I went in knowing he wasn't available. He wasn't mine. Complicating it more, his orders of spa services made it evident that he planned to do it all over again. And that excited me.

The lines between anger and happiness were blurry, too. I truly had no idea what to do. I wanted him to be mine. I wouldn't share him.

I watched him as I nibbled on the rest of my plate until he hung up the phone. He immediately started packing up his briefcase, before finally turning back to me.

"I'm going to have to get moving, but I will be back soon."

He walked over to me and I turned sideways in my chair.

"David will pack our things while you're out for us to leave after lunch."

He squatted down next to me.

My heart stopped. "You're leaving today?"

The desperation in my tone embarrassed me, but not Jonas. He stood and moved his legs between mine and smoothed my hair. I closed my eyes and without thought leaned my head against his stomach.

"This is okay, don't move away from me," Jonas assured.

I let out a long exhale as he continued to hold me to him.

"We'll discuss more of this later, but I've given this suite to a friend to … stay in. We'll be vacating this place this afternoon."

"Oh. How long will you be in town?" I said in a hushed tone.

"I don't know," Jonas purred as his fingers massaged my neck. "But that's also something I'm working on this morning, so I need to get going. I'll give you a call about setting up the lunch for four a little later."

He was being vague, which was unlike him.

"Who are we having lunch with?" I asked.

He stilled his hands. "With Paul and … Melissa."

I moved my head to look at him, so I could check to

see if he had completely lost his mind. "Jonas, what are you thinking? I don't want to have lunch with her, especially after what happened last night."

"It will be fine. She's going to be staying here. She's a great psychiatrist," Jonas said.

My mouth dropped open. He had definitely lost his mind.

"She won't be shrinking me," I argued. "She's way too tangled in—"

"I know that, Lily. I only said that to give some perspective on her capacity for understanding," Jonas said, pressing his lips lightly on my frown.

He was living in a dream world if he thought any woman would be understanding of him having sex with his ex. But then again, Dani and Ian were his best friends, and they were awfully understanding themselves.

"Perhaps," I conceded. And then, unable to help myself, I added, "Is she your friend, or companion?"

He eased away from me and walked over to the desk, picking up his coat and briefcase.

"Why do you keep asking me that?" He didn't wait for me to respond before adding, "Call me if you need me."

"Jonas?" I asked when we reached the door.

He paused in the gap, looking gorgeous, and my mind blanked for a few seconds.

I folded my arms. "She may understand, but I most certainly do not. I'd never want to share you with anyone. Ever. I'll have this lunch. And thank you for the spa. But I won't allow what happened last night to happen again. As long as she's yours, I … I won't be."

"No one I have ever been with, including Dani before our marriage, has ever made such demands on me," Jonas said. "I don't like to be pushed, Lily."

Not knowing how to respond, I turned on the balls of my feet and walked away in defiance. I heard the sound of the front door close with force just as I simultaneously closed the bathroom door behind me.

CHAPTER TWENTY

"MS. SALOMÉ? I'M Carrie," a young woman with a bright smile and tailored suit said.

"I'm here to take you down to the Guerlain Spa. Are you ready?"

I had just opened the suite door, approximately thirty minutes after Jonas left. Just as he had planned.

I was showered and dressed in a blue and white checked shirt, jeans that were looser than I remembered, and ankle boots. I imagined I wasn't her usual clientele in a designer tracksuit, but this wasn't something I had planned or packed for. All I could do was plaster a smile on my face to match hers.

"Lily, please," I said. "I'll just get my cellphone."

I quickly scanned the room for my handbag, spying my phone plugged into the computer on the desk. This must have been courtesy of Jonas, as I had completely forgotten to charge it myself. It was one more thing he has taken over, I thought as I rushed over to collect it.

Once we closed the door to the suite, I suddenly realized I didn't have a key to get back in. I looked down at my phone and sent Jonas a message, alerting him to my error, as I was too shy to ask Carrie about getting me a key. He sent back a text a few seconds later, alleviating my concern.

Carrie is aware, and will escort you back to the room. How are you feeling?

I couldn't help but smile as I texted back.

You only left me an hour ago. I'm fine. Just a little nervous.

He responded.

Don't be. The massage will do you good.

I followed Carrie to the elevators and sent another text as we waited in polite silence. *Thanks for this, but no more spoiling me. It makes me feel uncomfortable. Okay?*

He replied.

I know it does. But if I want you to have something, I'll give it to you. I would have given you a massage and saved you the discomfort, but I was told hands off.

I let out a groan.

"Everything alright, Lily?" Carrie asked, eyeing me questioningly as we climbed in the elevator.

"Yes. Sorry," I said and pretended to cough.

When we climbed out, I sent a message back.

Hands on if you're available. Hands off if you're taken.

He responded.

Just my hands? I think you enjoy more than my hands, according to your dream.

I covered a giggle that rose in my throat as we walked through the lobby.

Aren't you working, Mr. Crane?

He sent back.

I am. Answer.

I shook my head as I followed Carrie to the spa and stared down at the text. There was the Jonas I knew. He was ready to rule me, if I let him. I responded.

I do. You already know that. Now. I'm about to go in the spa.

Another message popped up.

Are you aroused? I bet you are. I would make you show me if I was there.

A tingle went through me. He was infuriating.

I pressed my lips together and wrote back.

I'm not. Stop, Jonas. I'm going into the spa.

Jonas answered.

We both know that's a lie. Stop pushing me and I'll stop.

My skin flushed and a flutter went through my stomach. I was pushing him, when I didn't really have the right. I had let him go. I sighed and decided to send one last message.

Great. You have me so turned on that I'll have to ask my massage therapist for a happy ending. Hope he's hot.

My phone vibrated once more. With a wicked grin, I turned it off and stuffed it in my pocket. I then felt a pang of guilt as we crossed into the beautiful glass and stone hall of the spa. I pulled my phone out to take one last glance at what he had said in response to that.

Nice try. I already reserved a woman. Enjoy and I'll see you in a couple of hours.

Jonas planned everything, of course. He didn't want Ian, or anyone else, touching me, but he seemed oblivious to my feeling the same way about him. It was infuriating.

Carrie turned me over to another smiling hostess that led me to a changing room to remove my clothing and put on a robe and slippers. After a quick change, I sat down on one of the plush chairs in a softly-lit lounge with a glass of champagne. This was living, I smiled to myself.

From there, I was led into a beautiful, dimly lit room where a female masseuse turned on meditative music. My worries and tense muscles went into her hands as she massaged honey vanilla lava oil into my skin. The warm oil and music lulled me into a peaceful sleep. Peaceful, because I had no ghost of my past invading them or thoughts of the problems I had waiting for me. There was only the bliss of being in Jonas's care and attention, which I had sorely missed.

He pressed his cock inside of me, and we moaned together at the incredible sensation of being joined together again. He pulled back and thrust deeper. I gasped and moved up to meet him. He started pumping in and out of me, first slow enough to make me whimper, then hard to make me cry out as the orgasm crest in me.

"Come," he demanded as he flexed and teased me.

Then he let go of my leg and slid his fingers on my clit. He played it like an instrument as he slammed against me until I came feverishly, clenching around his cock.

"Fuck," Jonas said.

His head fell back as he released hard inside me. He picked me up, and he was still hard as he carried us to the bed together.

"Jonas, stay with me," I said huskily.

He lowered me back on the bed.

"I'll never leave you."

"Miss? Your massage is done."

I jolted awake, suddenly unsure of my own surroundings. Another dream? Damn him.

I dried off and wrapped the robe around me. Exiting
the room, I was immediately handed another glass of
champagne, which I drank a bit too quickly. The alcohol
went straight to my head, and I floated on to a wax,
facial, manicure, and pedicure.

Changing back into my clothing, I peacefully went
back to the suite with Carrie, and she opened the door
for me. Before it closed, she had someone drop off a
couple of bags "complimentary" of the spa. I knew Jonas
had done this again, but I was too blissful to care. I
quickly sent a message to him.

*That was wonderful, and now I'm exhausted. Do I have time
for a nap?*

He wrote back.

A short one. I should be back in an hour.

I went straight into the bedroom and flopped down
on the freshly made bed. Before I reached REM, the
sound of the door opening and a movement assailed my
ears. Jonas had mentioned he wasn't going to stay in the
hotel. Was he running late?

A voice spoke loudly in the room. "Put the clothes in
here."

I sat up and watched Melissa Finch cross the doorway and stand in the bedroom. She looked stunning in a
designer black dress and stilettos. Her long, blonde hair

was perfectly styled in smooth waves. Her blue eyes narrowed, breaching her flawless profile as her attention settled on me.

"We need the bed changed, too."

"Yes, Ms. Finch," a bell person said as he rolled a cart in with a full set of high-end luggage.

I was wide awake now and tried to straighten up. I tightened my ponytail and smoothed my shirt in place.

"Hello, Melissa," I muttered.

She eyed me coolly. "Would you mind getting up? I need someone to come in here and get *our* room together."

My heart constricted and I stood up, following her command of me. *Their room. Jonas wasn't mine.*

"Sorry," I mumbled and stood as guilt crashed over me.

Whether Jonas was willing to acknowledge it or not, and whatever type of label he had for the two of them, he had cheated on Melissa with me.

"Dad didn't tell you to make her get up. He said he would do it."

Jonas's teenage son, Paul, said as he entered the room. He was a miniature version of Jonas with his dark wavy hair and chiseled face. His sea blues, like Jonas's, shone with mischievousness. His wide smile was all Dani. He did an overtly obvious assessment of me, and the corners of his mouth turned down.

"You're still hot, but you don't look so good."

Melissa laughed while my head tilted down and I

fidgeted with my feet. Out of the mouths of babes.

"I'm alright. Good … Good to see you again, Paul," I stuttered.

"I'd still date you in a heartbeat," he said and winked at me.

I let out a huff and folded my arms as he chuckled.

"I'd like both of you to go into the living room," Melissa said, bringing our attention to her.

I wasn't too happy with being ordered around like a child, and neither was Paul. He planted his feet and crossed his arms like he wouldn't be moved without force.

"One," he said. "I don't take orders from you. And this is my dad's suite, not yours." His snark was palpable. "Two, you're lucky I don't want to be in here with you either."

Melissa faced towards him. "Three," she chided. "You don't speak to me with disrespect. I'll have to mention your attitude to Jonas."

She scowled at Paul, but he smirked, apparently unfazed by her threat.

"*We* don't want to be in here with you anyway," Paul spoke for the two of us and motioned for me to follow.

I found myself chasing after him. My heart pounded in my chest as I passed by Melissa. I didn't know why, but I was afraid of her. I suppose because I had never had the experience of being the other woman.

Before I closed the door, she called out, "Get someone to change the bedding, now. It stinks in here."

CHAPTER TWENTY-ONE

"D ON'T MIND ME," Paul said, walking over to the couch and taking a seat. "I'm just here for the show." His face took on a cat-ate-the-cream look. "Dad was supposed to be back already, but you know how it is. When he has to work, he always runs late."

I listened for menace in his words, but didn't find it.

I glanced at him. "That must be hard."

"Yeah, but it's his thing," he said. "I have my music. My mom has her art and business. I do like him being around more, and he sends for me to come to him if he has to be away longer than he wants. I get a free vacation, and we get our time. Win-win."

I beamed at him and moved closer to the couch. "That's a great way to look at it.

He smirked. "I don't even know why I told you that. Mom and Dad said you have a way of getting people to tell you stuff. You should work for a tabloid or something. Sweet and pretty, no one would see you coming."

I giggled. "I don't know about that."

The little flirt. He would be a heartbreaker in a few

years.

"I didn't get you to blush? I'll have to try harder," Paul said with a lopsided grin.

The bedroom door opened behind us, and the sound of Melissa's heels hitting the uncovered hardwood floor startled me. Paul chuckled.

"I don't believe we formally met. I'm *Doctor* Melissa Finch, Jonas's girlfriend," she said, stopping in front of me.

Her red polished lips curved up into a beauty pageant-esque smile. I suppressed the blow at the mention of her being his "girlfriend" and plastered on my own smile, holding out my hand for her to take.

"Yes. You're right. I'm Lily, nice to meet you."

Her jeweled encrusted manicured hand limply shook the tips of my fingers.

Paul shook his head and laughed. "Surprise."

"Behave," Melissa said to Paul. She lifted her chin and walked over, sitting down on the couch next to Paul. "Take a seat, Lily."

I fidgeted and reluctantly walked over, taking the chair across from them. Where was Jonas?

"I'm sorry," I said. "I wasn't aware you were ... Jonas's girlfriend. I don't want to cause any trouble or anything...."

"Too late for that." She glared at me, then relaxed her face. "But you were aware that we were together before you came and spent the night in his bed. Correct?"

My cheeks heated to burning as I glanced between Paul and Melissa, not sure if I wanted to answer her enquiry in front of his son.

"I ... I ... Jonas came to my work," My words stumbled out as I consciously skipped over the last night in his bed part, though my face, which I was sure was scarlet, pretty much told everything.

She snorted. "So you jumped back into *my* boyfriend's bed because he came to pick you up from work?"

I pursed my lips. "I don't want to talk about this in front of Paul."

"If you knew Jonas, you'd know he's open and honest with his son. But that's not your style, right? You show up and then push him away and just when he's moving on, you come right back in to mess him up again."

My face fell. She was hitting every one of my insecurities. "Jonas insisted," I argued. "I didn't mean to mess up his life. He came to me as ... a friend."

"Jonas doesn't fuck friends," Melissa said bluntly.

My jaw dropped open at her crass words, though I was thrilled that she thought Jonas being intimate with me meant something.

"I'm not discussing this with you," I said, recovering.

Paul laughed and Melissa smirked.

"Oh, yes you are. I tried to speak with you before, after your betrayal with Ian, but you refused to listen. Instead, you went about trying to manipulate him by getting sick to keep him."

I tilted my head down in an attempt to avoid showing her how much her words affected me. I knew what she said wasn't true, but the way she said it had me questioning myself.

"That was low. Shut up, Melissa," Paul hissed at her.

"You don't tell me what to do," Melissa snapped back to him.

"Where the hell is Dad?"

Paul reached into his pocket and pulled out his phone, walking a few paces away from the couch.

Melissa turned her anger back on me. "Jonas has a tender heart, despite all he experienced with an absent mother and an unavailable father. He needed to explore his limits and gain some control over his life after his divorce. He sought a companion, someone willing to meet him where he was ready, but instead he found you. I told you as much before, but you didn't listen. I mean, why are you even here?"

"He insisted I stay with him while he's in New York, as his friend," I cleared my throat. "I was planning on going back to my place today. In Jersey City."

She rolled her eyes. "For his stay in New York, not beyond that. Right?"

I gave her a blank look and she stared at me as if I was daft. It then clearly occurred to her that perhaps I didn't know what she was eluding to, so she decided to enlighten me.

"Jonas doesn't just intend to visit for a week. He intends to relocate back to New York."

My jaw unhinged. I looked over at Paul, who didn't confirm or deny what she'd told me.

Instead, he said, "Dad's on his way, but he's missing the good stuff."

"I thought he discussed this with you. But then, you never really tell the truth and I don't know you well enough to know when you are lying," Melissa said with a wave of her hand.

I blinked and didn't answer.

"I heard about your little trouble, and, well, I have a friend in real estate here in New York. I can help you find a new place. I even have a friend that could let you rent her place today," she said.

I hunched my shoulders. "Did you hear me?" My voice raised. "I have my own place in Jersey City."

"Leave her alone, Melissa," Paul said, also raising his voice.

"Quiet, Paul," she snapped back, and curled her lips. "We can present the idea together to Jonas when he gets here."

I stood. Why Jonas hadn't shared his long-term plans was beyond me, but I wasn't going to spend another moment in her presence, let alone take her backhanded offer.

"No. I'm leaving."

Melissa cackled. "Running away again? I guess that's your pattern. I'll be sure to tell Jonas as much when he gets here."

Paul shook his head. "You can't leave. Dad will lose

it, and you don't want to be responsible for that, hmmm?" he asked with a grin.

I glared at him, and he chuckled.

Where had running away ever gotten me? No. I wasn't going to run this time. I lifted my chin as I turned my focus back to Melissa.

"You're right, Melissa. I have no right to be here, and I didn't know Jonas was staying in New York. If he is with you, this has nothing to do with me. As I said, I have my own place."

Melissa's face lit up and a wide grin spread across her face.

I folded my arms. Whatever happened I would stay. "However, I am going to wait and speak with Jonas."

Her smile eroded just as the door swung open and Jonas walked in with force.

"Dun dun dun dun, the plot thickens," Paul said, and laughed. "Damn it. No popcorn."

He leaned against the wall.

Jonas's eyes flashed to Melissa, who rose to walk over to him. "You told me you were hung up in arrivals at the airport, but Paul texted to tell me otherwise. Why didn't you call me?" He was met with silence as all the air left the room. "What's going on?"

"Don't I get a greeting?" Melissa asked and touched his arm.

Jonas's gaze shot to me, and I didn't disguise my hurt or hostility.

He stepped away from her and asked again, "What's

going on?"

"Melissa said you're her boyfriend and for Lily to stop fucking you," Paul chimed in.

Jonas's eyes flashed. "She what?" His anger filled the room, but I couldn't yet tell where it was directed. "Wait … Paul, go down to the car. I'll have David run you back home."

"Oh, come on, Dad. I don't want to leave. Hey, I can help out. She even offered up a friend of hers for Lily to stay with," Paul said, a little too much glee in his voice.

"That's enough," Jonas barked.

Paul shut his mouth, but didn't remove the grin on his face. Jonas pulled out his phone and made a call. His voice was the only sound in the room. Once he finished he turned back to his son.

"Sorry, Paul. We'll have our own day together this weekend. I promise," Jonas said.

"Don't sweat it, Dad. I understand you have your hands full. I can only hope to have the same trouble one of these days."

Jonas gave him a pained look. "I hope not, son. I'm sorry."

"It really is okay, Dad," Paul said in a moment of seriousness. He looked over at me. "I'm rooting for you, kid."

I blanched.

Paul snapped his fingers. "I was going for a blush. See ya."

Jonas hugged him and closed the door behind him.

"Now what the fuck is going on?" Jonas asked. "Sit down, both of you."

Melissa went dutifully over to her seat on the couch, but I wasn't ready to fall in line.

"I'd rather stand." I said.

His brow rose at me as he settled in the chair I had previously occupied.

"Just another example of her trying to control you," Melissa said.

Manipulating bitch. I conformed and went to take a seat. I sat on the couch and scooted as far away as I possibly could from Melissa.

"First of all," Jonas said tersely. "I don't know what you were thinking or why you would speak that way in front of my son. He is off limits." His eyes bore into Melissa's. "Don't ever, *ever* speak that way in front of him again."

"He would have found out anyway," she said.

"His finding out is *my* choice, not yours. You're *not* his mother, Dani is. And the two of us are raising him. Not you, Melissa. Not you."

Her hand trembled slightly as she smoothed her dress in place on her lap, the only evidence she was disturbed by his words. "Fine. I don't think that's healthy, but fine. You really can't blame me for being upset that you brought your ex back over and spent the night with her, though. You told me you would give us a try again."

"As companions," Jonas said. "We're not in a commitment, Melissa. You're not my girlfriend."

"Neither is she," Melissa said hotly.

"I'm not," I said. "I'm Jonas's friend, and I take responsibility for last night. Yes, I knew you were something. But I ... I wanted Jonas and I don't regret it."

I could feel his eyes on me.

"I don't either, Lily," Jonas said. "I wanted you, too."

"Jonas. I understand you having sex last night and I forgive you," Melissa said, breaking apart our moment. "But I still don't understand why she is here. I know you feel sorry for her, and she looks dreadful, so she might be a little sick, but really? She's so fragile. How could she manage to fit into your life? She's not from our circles. She can't possibly have experienced half the things I've done sexually with you. She can't handle or meet your needs. Hell, she was ready to run away before you came in."

I looked at Jonas, and my heart tumbled over at the pain and distress on his face.

"I didn't want to go. I didn't want to mess up your life. I didn't get sick on purpose to manipulate you. I got sick because ... because of Declan. And my parents. And everything. She's right, I've been weak. But I never wanted that to affect you. I pushed you away because I didn't want my problems to fall at your feet. I tried."

I wiped my face and gulped in air as my last words became incoherent. "I did what I did to protect you and everyone you and I care about. Because I ruin everything, and I didn't want to ruin you. I left out love, Jonas. Because I do love you."

I put my head in my hands. The seat next to me dipped and I felt Jonas's hand rubbing my back.

"There she goes again. Trying to manipulate you," Melissa chided.

"I'm surprised by you, Melissa. You of all people. A psychiatrist, a women's advocate," Jonas bit out.

Melissa jutted her chin. "I am, and I'm proud of that, but this is my personal life and our relationship. I love you, Jonas, and I believe in us. I relocated to Texas to be closer to you…."

"And I told you not to do that," Jonas said, his voice softening.

"I did it for us. I'm willing to compromise and meet your needs. I know you, your family, everything. She doesn't even know the half of it. What can she love? It's all lust or desperation for a hero to rescue her from her circumstances. That much I know for sure," Melissa said bitterly.

"Enough. Get out, Melissa," Jonas demanded, heat taking over his voice again.

"You told me you would give us a chance," Melissa pleaded once more, her voice now pained. "But for her, you're altering your life. That's not healthy for you or her. I'm very disheartened by your abrupt change, Jonas. And I believe I deserve more than just a call informing me you're basing yourself back in New York. It's not like you to act so impulsively."

We were all quiet for a moment then Jonas said, "Actually, I've been planning a return to New York for a while. Most of my business is here. I just moved the date forward. I don't want Lily going back to an apartment where she was violated. That's not healthy or safe."

He stroked my hair to let me know the latter part of his speech was for me. I didn't answer, as I was too overwhelmed to say anything. When he continued, his focus returned to Melissa.

"As for us—"

"Stop, Jonas." Melissa said. "We can talk about this in private."

Jonas snorted. "There is no more privacy," he said sardonically. "I didn't invite you to Texas or New York. You came all on your own. I offered my suite at your disposal today out of kindness. Yet you spit on that hospitality and have now not only insulted Lily, but you did so in front of my son."

"I'm sorry, Jonas," Melissa looked down at her hands.

"Say it to Lily," Jonas said in a curt tone.

Her mouth twisted. "No. I wouldn't mean it. You deserve better than she will ever be able to give you," she said, looking up and meeting his eyes.

"Like you?" Jonas said with snark. "No. I want Lily."

Tears began rolling down my cheeks as I took in his words.

"Jonas, please," Melissa said nasally. "I came here because I want us to be together. Think about how I feel, you moving in with your ex-lover."

"Moving in?" I mumbled.

"Melissa," Jonas said, exasperated. "I'm not helping Lily to hurt you."

"You could help her and not live with her," Melissa said irritably. "Surely, you understand my concern. She will just run off again, and where will you go? Right back to me, like the last time."

There was a hint of double meaning in the way she said "last time." I stilled next to Jonas.

"I didn't have sex with you, last time or this time," Jonas said. I leaned into his side and his head rested atop mine for a few seconds. "But like I told you on the phone last night—"

"I'm not ready to give up on us," she cut him off bitterly. "You're not answering all the issues I raised because you're worried, too, and you should be. She is a baby, Jonas. You can't be serious—"

"And you're not listening." His voice was unsteady. "Fine, if you won't leave, we will," Jonas said, rising from his seat. "But you need to find somewhere else to stay. My space is no longer available to you."

He took my hand and I eased to my feet. He leaned over to my ear as if to give us a semblance of privacy.

"We'll talk this out. All of it, but damn it, you're not leaving me." Jonas's voice broke. He took my face in his hands that were trembling. "Please don't leave or disappear from my life again. I can't … bear it."

His eyes bore into mine, and I was overcome with

the desperation I found there. His pain and fear were laid out before me. Out of love for this man, I had to answer it. I put all my feeling into my next words to him.

"I won't. No matter what, I won't. I'm here for you, for us."

He pulled me hard to him, crushing my body against his. "I choose you. I want you, know that. I care. God, I feel, I care. Oh, Lily." He kissed me tenderly on the lips. "Trust that. We can work with that. Trust me."

"I do, Jonas. I do," I choked.

Melissa started crying audibly next to us. In our moment, I had forgotten she was there. Even though she had been awful to me, my heart ached for her because I knew exactly what she was losing.

Jonas breathed me in. "I'll meet you down by the car. Okay?"

I trusted him, and nodded in compliance. He cupped my face in his hands again and pressed his lips to my forehead, then let me go. I walked to the closet and took out my coat and handbag. I glanced behind me and saw Jonas sitting down next to her. His arm was around her shoulder, providing her the comfort she needed. A pang went through my chest, but I walked out of the suite.

I rode the elevator down to the lobby and walked outside, where I found David by the car out front. He handed me a handkerchief. I wiped my tear-streaked face and sat down in the back of the car.

After about fifteen minutes, I saw Jonas walking to-wards us, his face solemn. David opened the door. Jonas sat down next to me and sighed. I reached for him and climbed into his lap. We didn't mention Melissa, but her presence was there. He tucked me under his chin and stroked his hand over my back. I settled into the comfort that came with us wrapped in each other's arms.

My phone chimed, then chirped with an incoming message. Fear walked across my heart, Declan? Jonas held me close, reminding me I wasn't alone anymore. I snuggled in closer.

Dani once told me if I let Jonas in, he would move his world for me. And in this moment, I believed her. Holding that thought in my heart, clinging to it as a shield against whatever we were met with next, I knew I would give myself to him completely.

Tiger Lily Part Three
available now.

ACKNOWLEDGMENTS

Thank you to Alan, my husband, best friend and partner. I love you.

Thank you to the team that helped me with Tiger Lily Part Two. I greatly appreciate your help.

Thank you to Leah Campbell.

Thank you to Amanda Dawson.

Thank you to Donna Rich.

Thank you to Silvia Curry of Silvia's Reading Corner

Special thanks to Hermione, Rod, and Tammy for beta reading.

Thank you to Cassandra for her assistance with the blurb.

Thank you to Paul Salvette.

Thank you to all the bloggers and reviewers.

Thank you to the readers for reading my story. I most sincerely hope you enjoyed it.

ABOUT THE AUTHOR

Amélie S. Duncan writes contemporary, erotic romances with a dark edge. Her inspiration comes from many sources including her life experiences and travels. She lives on the West Coast of the United States with her husband.

47422156R00148

Made in the USA
Middletown, DE
23 August 2017